BANISHED

BECA LEWIS

Published by:
Perception Publishing
https://perceptionpublishing.com

This book is a work of fiction. All characters in this book are fictional. However, as a writer, I have, of course, made some of the book's characters composites of people I have met or known.

Table of Contents

Prologue

A sea of bodies swayed in time to the words that flowed over them. Words that made them forget about their daily lives, if only for a moment. Each word was carefully chosen as if it was a note in a symphony. Each word designed to sway hearts, minds, and ultimately control lives.

The crowd no longer cared about, or had forgotten, the meaning of the words. They were lost in the feelings. Emotions moved through them, first building them up and then letting them down in perfect timing.

They were one organism with one goal, one intent, one ruler, one God. They had no thoughts of their own. They were servants to their new master, and joy filled their hearts because they were a chosen people.

The Preacher was pleased. His plans were working. Years of learning how to manipulate emotions in a crowd were paying off. It was almost effortless now. He was a master at playing the audience with the rhythm and pitch and sound of words as they flowed like honey from his mouth. Or hit like bullets when he wanted them to. Then he would comfort the people, and assure them that he knew what they wanted, what they needed, and he could give it to them.

Sometimes it wasn't so easy. The Preacher would lose his focus for a moment, and project forward into where he knew it would all lead. But it was his focus that was playing the crowd, and the moment he lost it, they would be bewildered until he returned to lead them.

What he said was far less important than how he said it. Standing tall on the platform set in the middle of the Market, he was a beam of dark light. His face hidden inside the cowl of the black cloak he wore, no one in the crowd could have said what he looked like.

But they were always sure when he was near. They knew what he felt like. They knew what he stood for. They knew what he could do, and they loved him for that power. They knew that if they followed him and what he preached, they would be happy forever.

Behind the Preacher stood seven dark columns of men, their faces also hidden so that they too remained anonymous. However, who they were was not a secret. They were the Kai-Via, the Seven. The enforcers.

The Seven scanned the crowd, looking for those who were not swaying in response to the words—looking for the outsiders, the Mages, the ones who hadn't yet fallen in love with the message.

The Kai-Via's role as enforcers wasn't needed as much anymore. The crowds had been tamed. Even this crowd. And when they were finished here, the one true religion would have taken over the planet of Thamon.

Everyone who hadn't succumbed to the power of the Preacher's words was being eliminated. They had been banished. Forever.

However, the head of the Kai-Via watched as the Preacher used his words to reinforce and sustain what they had already done, and wondered whose side the Preacher was on. He would be watching.

As the Preacher spoke, the crowd bowed their heads, and fell to their knees in gratitude because everything they wanted was theirs, as long as they followed the God, Aaron.

The wind whipped through the crowd, blowing shawls and cloaks into the air like flags. Many of the converted wore black robes like the Kai-Via, the Seven, but their robes didn't have hoods. There was no hiding for them. Each face registered in the minds of the seven men scanning the crowd. Looking for those who were too alert. Too interested in things other than the speaker and the words that he spoke.

A sea of black robes was a powerful sight to see, and the Preacher and the Kai-Via reveled in the knowledge that this crowd was theirs as were the thousands of crowds across Thamon. Each crowd full of the young, the old, men, and women, all gathered as one, worshipers of the one God that ruled them all.

The Preacher was the mouthpiece of that one God. He delivered the message. The Preacher gathered them all into the emotions of oneness, togetherness, and sameness. And as his words ebbed and flowed, the crowd roared in approval.

For them, magic was dead. Aaron was the ruler. They were his subjects, and for them life was now glorious. What they had before was gone. All their worries were replaced with certainty. All they had to do was follow their new religion of Aaron-Lem, and all would be well.

Anyone who had resisted the Aaron-Lem doctrines had been killed or rounded up and placed in prisons where everything they ever believed was sucked out of them, and replaced with the laws of the one true religion. Or they had died in protest.

The time of Aaron's rule was upon them, and they thought

they were happy.

At the back of the crowd stood a man and a woman. There was nothing different about them. Their faces registered the same joyful emotions. They swayed in time to the words. They bowed their heads along with everyone else.

But hidden in the folds of their black robes, their fingers touched. They knew something that the Preacher and the Seven did not know, or at least did not want to believe.

Magic was not dead. Aaron was not their God. And they were not alone.

One

Meg stole a look over her shoulder, checking to see if anyone had followed her. The need to find shelter before nightfall was becoming more and more imperative. Night on this planet was doing something to her, something she couldn't control.

Time was running out. Thamon's second sun, Trin, was setting, and the night was chasing at her heels. She needed to find the building she was looking for soon while Etar, Thamon's first sun, still gave her enough light to see.

As Meg ran through the shadows, she told herself that she had to stop worrying. She would get to the building in time, and she would be safe for the night.

However, constantly looking over her shoulder was slowing her down, and she felt like an idiot for being so paranoid. But the habit of being afraid was hard to shake.

Stop it, Meg said to the voice in her head that kept telling her she was in danger, not only from the present but from her past. Someone might find her.

But that was impossible. No one knew where she had gone, and even if they did, they would never find her. Besides, even if they were looking right at her, they wouldn't know who she was. Because she could be anyone, or anything, any time she wanted to—most of the time.

But that was a secret, and a problem she was going to keep to herself until she could find others like her. Or at least someone that she could trust. In the meantime, she had no intention of shapeshifting unless she had to. It was too dangerous. Because she had made a massive mistake, and there was no one to blame for it but herself.

So, for now, she made herself look like any other inhabitant of the city of Woald. If anyone were paying attention to her, she would be a nondescript woman wearing the standard clothes of the people living on the Islands. Which meant she needed to slow down and look like them, not like someone trying to hide.

Breathe, she told herself. She had been in worse scrapes than this. Well, maybe not.

What had happened was not what she had planned. Running away from home was meant to be an escape to where she could be free. But she had moved too quickly without thinking things through. Not that unusual for her, but back home someone always helped her when she made rash decisions and stupid mistakes. However, when she overheard her parents discuss their plans to move her someplace she wouldn't be so dangerous to others and herself, she panicked.

There was no way she was going to conform and become a good girl or good shapeshifter. Getting into trouble was too much fun. So that night, while they slept, she ran away. It was surprisingly easy. When you can turn yourself into anything, there is nowhere you can't go and nothing you can't do—if you're careful.

And she had learned to be careful. At least about that. What she wasn't careful about was where she was going. It hadn't taken her long to figure out that she had moved too quickly.

By the end of the first week on her own, she had discovered

her mistake, but it was too late to do anything about it. Thamon was her new home, and she would have to find a way to like it.

She could have chosen to go to another dimension on Gaia, but instead, she decided to leave the planet altogether. It was a big universe, and she wanted to explore. The only place she didn't want to go was where her parents were planning to take her, so instead, she talked one of the portal makers into sending her to someplace else. Well, she didn't talk him into it, she scared him into it by threatening to tell a secret she knew about him.

He had told her he would send her to the perfect place for shapeshifters like her. She believed him. To be fair, he was telling the truth. Because he probably wanted her to go someplace where they controlled people like her, and to a place that she could never leave. She had thought he meant it would be a place where she could be free. What he meant was it was a place where others would be free of people like her. What he had done was banish her to a place that hated people like her.

She supposed she shouldn't have threatened the portal maker. The sad part was, she didn't know a secret about him, but then, he didn't know that.

At first, Meg thought she had arrived in paradise. Although it was only two islands connected with a land bridge, it was beautiful, and much like home with meadows and forests. What made it different were the two suns, Etar and Trin.

Meg spent her first days celebrating her newfound status as a free woman on a beautiful planet. There was no one to tell her what to do. She was independent for the first time in her life. Because she could look like anyone, she fit in where ever she went. Life was easy. She stole food and supplies or sweet-talked the unsuspecting into giving her what she needed or wanted.

And she listened. It was what she began to hear that changed everything. She discovered the reason why the portal maker had sent her here. She could be relatively free, but only if no one suspected what she was. So far, she had been lucky, and she was going to keep it that way.

Trying to keep herself from looking afraid because that would give her away, Meg turned the last corner and found the building she had seen earlier in the day. It looked deserted, a place to settle in and decide what to do.

She couldn't let herself wish she had never run away. Or think about the fact that she would have been better off staying with her parents and letting them take her where they had planned. It was too late to feel sorry for herself. There was no way to go home. Thamon was her home now, and she was going to make the best of it.

There had to be others like her. She would find them before the wrong people found her. Because what the rulers of Thamon had in mind for people like her didn't sound like anything she wanted to experience. Luckily, they didn't know about her, and she was going to keep it that way.

Two

At the first sign of dawn, the problem Meg experienced at night slipped away, and she felt safe enough to leave the building in search of food and information. The Market was Meg's first stop each morning.

As soon as the faintest beam of light streaked through the sky from Thamon's first sun, farmers and craftspeople would roll their carts into the Market to set up their booths and stalls. One minute the Market was empty, and the next it would be filled with multiple colorful mini-stores and booths selling almost anything the people of the Islands might want.

All of this set up took place in Etar's pale blue light. Even though it was one of Thamon's suns, Etar was far enough away to be not much brighter than the reflected light of the moon on Meg's home planet Gaia. To Meg, it made the mornings on Thamon as magical as the twilight that she had loved at home.

The first booth that Meg went to every morning served her new favorite drink. It tasted like coffee, but better. Not quite as bitter, but not sweet either. Because it was made from a bean that looked like a coffee bean from back home, Meg wondered if they were related.

The young man working the booth always filled her cup to

the brim and gave her at least two slices of the delicious bread that they sold there. Meg never paid, and he never noticed. If he had, he wouldn't have minded.

Charming people into giving her what she wanted was so easy for Meg, the fun of it had faded long ago. But she didn't have any money, and she was not prepared to work at a job, so Meg felt that charming or stealing what she needed was her only option.

To get her free morning meal, all she had to do was make herself look a little more like the kind of woman the young man favored. Just enough to catch his eye, but not enough to be too visible to the rest of the people at the Market.

It had taken her only one quick peek inside of his mind to know what he liked. She had stayed inside his head only long enough to get the information she needed. Unless she had to, she never lingered inside anyone's mind.

Part of it was because Meg tried not to do more magic or manipulation than was necessary to get what she wanted or needed. But there was another reason for her short stays. She had discovered that most minds were so full of junk and bits of nonsense, it felt like stepping into a pile of trash.

However, in spite of not feeling any guilt for the way she got what she wanted, Meg was grateful for what she received. In return, she tried to leave most people feeling better about themselves as a thank you.

Meg smiled at the young man as he passed her the food and drink, and decided what he needed was a companion. If she ran across his match, she promised herself she would introduce them to each other.

As Meg sat at a small table at the edge of the Market enjoying her breakfast, she told herself that it was probably a mistake going to his cart every morning. But she needed something that felt familiar with all the uncertainty of this new world. Meg stayed watching the crowd for a while, but by the time Trin had risen above the horizon, she had slipped away into the crowd of people who had arrived to shop in the Market.

As she walked, she continually tweaked her look enough to disappear, but being careful never to change so much it would be noticeable. It was a delicate balance, and she was always on the lookout for others doing the same thing.

There have to be more people like me, Meg thought. The trouble was, they could be anywhere, or anything. Well, anything that moved. Meg couldn't turn herself into a tree, or stone. But the lizard sunning himself on the rock could be someone like her. Unlikely though. She had never met another shapeshifter who could be almost anything. Even her parents didn't have the range that she did, and her sister, Suzanne, could only turn into a dragon. A funny-looking one at that, but still a dragon.

What Meg wanted to do first was find others like herself. She hoped to learn more about what the members of Kai-Via had in mind for Mages and shapeshifters, and how to avoid their detection. All she had learned so far was that it was dangerous to be a Mage or shapeshifter in Thamon. But why? And how dangerous? She decided that she might find out more answers today because the Preacher was arriving that afternoon to speak at a gathering at the Market. Everyone was excited. They had heard that he was mesmerizing.

Meg wasn't sure that was a good quality, even though she used it to her own advantage all the time.

Just a moment before, she had snitched a new shawl off a cart owned by an old woman by simply manipulating what the woman was seeing. Meg had been admiring the shawl for days, and finally, she couldn't resist. But seconds later, reason had kicked in, and a newly found caution made her put it back. It was such a beautiful shawl someone might recognize it, and then she would be in trouble.

Besides, she had to admit she had felt sorry for the woman. If she were going to steal, it would have to be from someone who could afford it or deserved it. And of course, too many things going missing would make the spies of the Kai-Via suspicious. That was the last thing she needed.

Instead, she wrapped her plain gray cloak around her and strolled through the Market, listening, and observing, passing the time until the Preacher arrived.

What Meg didn't notice was someone else was doing the same thing, but their focus was on her.

Three

Wren reluctantly turned away from watching the woman and headed to the daily morning meeting. Roar and Ruth were probably already there waiting for her. If she were too late, they would start to panic, thinking something might have happened to her, and she didn't want them to go through that.

She knew how that felt. Disappearances happened almost every day. Friends vanishing without a trace. So even though their little group made sure that they held their meetings in one of the deserted homes located on Hetale, Lopel's sister island, they had become even more cautious. They adjusted their appearances as needed, just in case someone was watching. As watchers themselves, they were all too aware of how easy it was to observe and not be seen.

Wren and her friends had learned that there was no such thing as being overly cautious. More than one member of their group had disappeared since they started holding meetings.

It was possible that someone had tracked them to a meeting, and had told the Kai-Via about them. Of course, multiple other things could have happened, but now, to be safe, every few days they moved to a new meeting place.

This morning they were in their latest location, a deserted

home just on the outskirts of the town of Tiwa. They didn't break in. The houses were already open. In fact, these homes looked as if their owners would return at any moment. Nothing was broken or taken. Only the occupants were gone, almost as if they had vanished into thin air.

So far, Wren's group had met in many deserted homes. There was never a shortage, and there were more places for them to choose from every day. But the fact that people were disappearing was something never discussed in public. Wren knew that it was not because no one cared. It was because they had been told not to notice. And if for some reason they did notice, everyone was too afraid to say anything.

The people of the Islands were not accustomed to being afraid. For centuries they had lived in an isolated peace. Now the Kai-Via had come to the Islands and changed everything.

On three sides of Lopel and its sister island Hetale, towering white cliffs led down to the sea. From the cliffs, each Island sloped gently down to the Arrow, the land bridge that connected the two islands.

During big storms that stretch of land would be underwater, but most of the time it remained an open passageway. The locals called it the Arrow because it was as straight as an arrow, and looked as if it was pointing at each Island. It also provided easy access to the beaches.

For the non-magical inhabitants of Lopel, the cliffs were impossible to navigate, but there were beautiful white sand beaches below them.

So Mages had long ago carved a long series of steps into the sides of cliffs. Now the beaches below the cliffs were accessible to everyone alike, magical or not, if you didn't mind climbing up and down stairs. Otherwise, the Arrow was the easier route.

Because the Arrow connected Lopel and Hetale, during

the warm months, a local tradition was to sit on the beach on Hetale in the morning and watch Etar rise in the east as Trin moved towards it, having risen in the west. For the people of Lopel and Hetale, their favorite time to watch the suns was when they passed each other directly overhead.

Until the Kai-Via arrived, everyone would stop and watch the passing hoping to catch sight of the blue flash that sometimes happened. If it did, it was considered a good omen. But that was magical thinking, and therefore now banned on all of Thamon.

There was constant travel between the two islands either by sea or by using the Arrow. The islanders traveled to visit relatives and friends but also to trade goods and services. During the warm months when storms were rare, the Market that Meg visited was located on the Arrow. It extended from one end of the Arrow to the other, often spilling over onto the Arrow's narrow beaches where fishermen would bring in their daily catch.

Because of the easy access to each other, there were many blended families on both islands. But other than that they were isolated from the rest of Thamon, and they liked it that way.

Sometimes a ship would arrive carrying goods from other parts of Thamon, and everyone would flock to the docks to see what the ships had brought. They asked about the rest of Thamon, but unless the news affected trade, there was little that worried the people of Lopel and Hetale.

When the Kai-Via and the Preacher arrived on the island of Hetale, everything had changed. It wasn't noticeable at first.

The people of Lopel and Hetale were tolerant and supportive of all beliefs, so when the Kai-Via talked about the religion that they represented, no one questioned it. They simply listened and either agreed or disagreed. There was no judgment placed on what they heard.

The men who called themselves the Kai-Via built a Temple on Hetale, and left it open for anyone to visit. They held daily services, and people started attending out of curiosity. The rumor spread that the Preacher was amazing to listen to, and that they always felt happy after the services.

Soon the doctrine of Aaron-Lem started finding its way into conversations between the people of both islands, and those conversations began to be heated ones. When more and more people from Hetale began to miss the daily rising and crossings of the suns, the people on Lopel started to worry.

To those that were paying attention, the number of people converting to what was preached in the Temple was shocking. Especially considering how quickly the lives of people on both Islands had changed. To Wren's group and others like her, not for the better.

It turned out they were right to worry. The people who were disappearing were not a random mix of people. They were people like them—those with magical skills, the Mages and shapeshifters.

As Wren neared the meeting place, she dropped down into the branches of a tree in the backyard, fluffed her feathers, and then, turning into a lizard, climbed down the tree and under the door of the house. It was only when she was sure that it was safe, that she transformed back into the woman who had been watching Meg.

Four

The man known as the Preacher walked down to the Arrow to watch Etar rise from the east and turn the land and the seas that surrounded the Islands a light blue. It was his favorite time of day. It always had been, even back home in Oreth. Life had been so easy then. No one expected anything of him. He was like all the boys in his village. They would play until Trin rose in the west. That meant it was time to return home to do their chores before heading to school, or the farm, depending on what time of year it was.

A few rocks jutted out of the sand, providing material for someone to turn them into benches. Ibris didn't want to think about the fact that it was probably a magical gift that had enabled someone to make a place for him to sit. He filed it away into the part of his brain that couldn't make sense of the path he had chosen.

Instead, he sat with an ease that belied the unease that he felt. The stone bench on the beach was his favorite spot on Hetale. From there he could watch the ever-changing sea and all the comings and goings on the Arrow. He watched as the Market filled up with vendors preparing to sell their wares as they did every day during the warm months.

Back home in Oreth, the Market was held only at the end of the week when everyone from the surrounding countryside would gather in the town's square. Its intended purpose was to sell goods and services, but everyone knew that the conversations that took place were why it was such a favorite thing to do.

During the cold months, Ibris thought he would go crazy waiting for the days when he would have more than his immediate family to talk to. Inside their home waiting for the cold to be over, they would be warm and safe, but there were only so many books to read, or games to play around the large dining room table before he would slowly go crazy. He needed people. He loved watching the people of his village interacting with each other.

Now he watched the Market on the Islands instead of the people of his village. It was his habit of observation that told him that although on the surface it appeared as if nothing had changed at the Market, he knew that his preaching was having an effect.

This made him both proud and sad. Proud that he was able to do what was asked of him, sad because he missed the easy babble of the Market that had reminded him of home. Yes, there were still conversations going on. But they were contained. The ability to say whatever they wanted to say without worry had disappeared. These people knew there were consequences for not accepting Aaron-Lem as the one true religion.

In his sermons, Ibris told them that the consequences were all good. They were a blessed people chosen to learn the ways and rules of Aaron-Lem. Flowing with the one true God of Aaron-Lem, they would have more of everything that they wanted.

Except Ibris knew what the real consequences were, and he

tried not to care. After all, he was the Preacher of the most elite of the Kai-Via. The Kai-Via were Aaron-Lem's missionaries, trained by Stryker, Aaron's right-hand man. And Ibis and this Kai-Via were considered the most powerful and effective of them all.

The Islands were not the first place Ibris had transformed in the name of Aaron-Lem. But they were the first ones where he had managed to convince Stryker that he could convert the people without bloodshed. And Stryker agreed that he could try.

However, if Ibris didn't succeed, then it wouldn't be the Kai-Via that the people would fear, it would be Aaron's Warrior Monks waiting in the wings to be put to use. Ibris had seen what that looked like, and he never wanted to see it again. Stryker would say Ibris was going soft. It was not the way of Aaron-Lem. Therefore it could not be his way. They had to do whatever it took to convert the people and stop those that opposed them.

Stryker gave Ibris the warm season to accomplish his blood-free mission. Ibris prayed he could do it. He had seen enough death.

Shaking himself free of the thoughts of the past, Ibris reminded himself that he only had until Trin rose to observe the Market, and then he was expected back in the Temple to deliver his morning sermon.

He would also be preaching again in the Market later that day, which meant that he would be expected to manipulate minds twice today. He had to prepare for the fact that he would probably be sick that night, drained. Depending on how much work it took, he could also end up with a massive headache and nausea.

He needed all the sustenance he could get from the rising Etar. It had worked for him as a child, and he needed it to work for him as an adult. It bothered him that his thoughts always returned to childhood on days like this. It was dangerous.

Ibris had never dreamed of becoming the man who did Stryker's bidding and preached a religion, any religion. He had never been interested in the gods. Instead, he had loved the farming life, following his father and brothers into the fields each morning during the warm months.

His sisters stayed home with his mother preparing the days' meals and working in the gardens. Every night that they could, they would eat their evening meal outside during Thamon's two sunsets. It was considered holy time. The time they would bow their heads and thank the God, Zuien, for giving them light and heat. That was all he knew about the gods. It had been enough.

These were dangerous thoughts for him to have, and he knew it. If Aaron-Lem, represented by Stryker, was as all-mighty as he claimed to be, he could read Ibris' mind when he was unprotected and find his desire to return home. And if he did, he would punish him. So far, he had been lucky. Either his defenses were strong enough, or Stryker wasn't looking. Ibris was reasonably sure it was because Stryker wasn't looking, for now.

Besides, he couldn't go back. Ever. His home and his family were gone. It was Stryker who had saved him from the same fate but doomed him to another, giving him this mission that he was not allowed to fail. Stryker would say that he had saved Ibris' soul. Stryker had taught him the ways and means of using words, spoken, and unspoken, to bring people into the arms of Aaron-Lem.

Ibris sighed and watched the market fill. No one would know who he was because they had never seen his face. The only people who knew him were the other members of the Kai-Via, Aaron, and Stryker.

All the people knew of him was his voice and his words.

If he had to speak now, he would alter his voice not to be recognized, and Ibris never used the power he had while revealing himself in public.

As he turned to go, Ibris thought he got a glimpse of someone he hadn't seen before. But when he looked again, he didn't see her. That was the problem. They could be anyone. And that was what he and the Kai-Via were here to stop.

Five

"I saw that woman again today," Wren said. She didn't need to tell Roar and Ruth who she meant. They had been taking turns watching her.

The newcomer had arrived in Woald a week before. No one knew where she had come from, but they suspected that it was not from Thamon because at first she had been so disoriented it was almost comical to watch. She was startled by everything—from the two suns to the way people dressed.

At first, the newcomer was not careful, probably because she had no idea the danger she was in. Not wanting her to be taken immediately by the Kai-Via, the three friends had staged a conversation just for her to hear.

They had strolled into the market, looking as if they were three men from the Island of Hetale. It didn't take long to find her even though she had once again altered her appearance, which made them even more sure she was one of them.

She was sitting at a table eating lunch, staring at the food as if she had never seen anything like it before.

Wren, Ruth, and Roar bought food from a vendor and then sat at a table as close to her as they could. They had taken a chance doing what they did because someone else might be watching. But they spoke very quietly, hoping she was as observant as she needed to be if she was what they suspected.

They were rewarded for their efforts when they felt her attention turn to them. Either she was a spy for the Kai-Via or a stranger to Thamon.

Not entirely sure which one she was, they were careful with what they said. They talked about the people who were disappearing from Hetale. The three friends mentioned that it appeared that the ones who were missing were the Mages and shapeshifters. When Roar added that the shapeshifter community was disappearing the fastest, the woman turned her full attention to them. They had struck a nerve.

The three of them nodded their heads in agreement, and Ruth said the words that they hoped the woman would understand. "Well, the shapeshifters could have disappeared like the Mages, or they could still be here since they could be anyone."

The woman jerked back as if in shock, and her drink spilled over her hand. As she wiped it off, the three friends got up from the table and went separate directions, disappearing as soon as they could into another form. As far as they knew they were the only three shapeshifters left on the Islands, unless their shapeshifter friends had found a way to disappear.

If that were true, they wished their friends would come back. There was no way they were going to stop the Kai-Via on their own. They needed help, which is why they were watching the newcomer so closely. If she was what she appeared to be, they needed her. It had been a week now. Perhaps it was time to test her.

"She spends her nights in one of the deserted buildings on the outskirts of Woald. We could talk to her then," Roar suggested.

"Is that safe?" Ruth asked. "First, if we have noticed her, it is possible that the Kai-Via have noticed her too, and are using her as bait to catch us."

"It's true," Wren answered. "She could be bait. She might even be doing it on purpose. Although her confusion seems pretty real. Either way, it could be a trap."

"Or it could be dangerous because she is dangerous," Ruth said. "We haven't seen what she can do. What if she turns against us before we have a chance to explain who we are?"

Wren shot the answer right back. "Oh, come on. We can get to her without being in danger. What have we become, a group of wimps? If we wait much longer, the Kai-Via will discover her for sure, and we'll lose our chance. We have to move on this now."

A mumble of agreement went around the room. Wren was usually right, but that didn't mean they always had to agree with her. They were a mixed bunch. No one would ever have thought the three of them were friends, let alone people who would put themselves at risk by trying to stop the Kai-Via.

They were very careful. They had rules. The first rule was that when they were alone together, they had to appear in their "true" form. There was more than one reason for that precaution. First, it was for their benefit. Since any of them could change into any moving being, there was a fear among shapeshifters like them that eventually they would not be able to return to their true selves. So having to shift back for meetings kept them in practice.

The other reason was for the groups' protection. They needed to be sure that the person sitting across from them was their friend and not a shapeshifter who had taken on their form. Someone could, but it would be hard to maintain. Besides, they shared a secret that kept them positive that they were who they appeared to be when they met.

Even though Wren was the un-elected leader of the group, she was still a young woman. Roar was an older man who knew Wren's story but had promised not to tell anyone. If and when it was necessary, Wren would do the telling, no one else.

Ruth, the third member, was an older woman who had lived on Hetale, but once she heard the Preacher she knew what it would lead to and went looking for Roar and Wren before the Kai-Via came looking for her. She, too, yielded to Wren's leadership because Roar said they would be safe if they did.

"Okay, tonight," Wren said. "Roar, you watch her just in case she doesn't come to the building. Ruth and I will wait inside until she gets there or you come to tell us where she went.

"A cat seems like a good choice, don't you think?" Roar said.

The other two laughed. Roar loved being cats. It was how he got his name. He had tried many times to be a lion but had never accomplished it. House cats were as far as he got.

Wren smiled to herself, thinking that Roar should have been called, Meow. All three of them laughed again at the thought. They took joy when and wherever they could.

Six

Ever since Meg heard the three men talking in the market, she had looked for them again. Something was off about the whole thing. She didn't believe in coincidences. Like what happened with the portal maker. It wasn't a coincidence that he sent her to Thamon. He sent her here on purpose because she mistreated him. Not just that one time, every time she used his services.

Only now, alone in a strange, and apparently dangerous place, did Meg begin to understand what her older sister kept trying to tell her while they were growing up. Meg could still hear her sister's voice in her head. Suzanne would say over and over again that a gift didn't make you superior; it made you more responsible. Meg hadn't believed it then, and she still wasn't sure she believed it now. But her feeling superior was the reason she had mistreated the portal maker, and look at how he got his revenge.

If she ever got back home, he would have some explaining to do. Meg didn't think he was too worried about it. If she even survived Thamon, she would have to find a portal maker, if there was such a thing here, and they would have to know the exact coordinates of where she came from. Yes, pretty much impossible. So whether she liked it or not, she was now a resident of the planet Thamon, and at least for now, the city of Woald.

Then there were the three men. Not trying to hurt her, but trying to warn her. They didn't just show up and start talking about something that would impact her if she wasn't careful. That meant that somehow they had noticed her, and had an idea what she could do. She was lucky. It could have been someone else who saw her, someone who, from what the three men said, didn't like magic.

She needed to be more careful and less noticeable. And she needed to find the three men. But she had no idea where to look. She was also acutely aware that she didn't actually know how to act normal. What did normal people do? How did they manage to look like just one thing all the time? What was an ordinary life?

For a week now Meg had been studying the people who passed through the Market, wondering if any of them had magical skills. Where she came from everyone did, not that she had paid much attention to them. Because everyone's gifts were different, and Meg considered some more important than others. To Meg, the ability to become anyone was the highest and best magical skill. Everything else was secondary. But right now, she would be happy to find just one person with the tiniest bit of magic.

Hours had gone by since her breakfast, and Meg was hungry again. She spotted a booth that had a long line in front of it and thought that must mean they had good food. At first, she stood in line like everyone else, trying to be patient as everyone took their turns stepping up to the window to order. It didn't go well.

Within a few minutes, she was fidgeting with impatience, and people started to turn to look behind them to see who was jiggling the line. With a sigh, Meg stepped out of line and into the crowd. Slipping behind the food booth, she wrapped her gray cloak around her, squatted down behind a garbage can, and changed into a raven.

The raven walked behind the lines of trash cans, came out the other side, and took off into the air. It swooped around the Market and saw a table where one of the men who had been in the front of the line had just laid his newly purchased food. When he turned to see if his friend was following him, the raven landed on the table, snatched the food, and flew away.

It was all over within seconds. As Meg flew out of the marketplace, carrying her newly acquired lunch, she giggled to herself at how easy that had been. The idea that she needed to be careful, act normal, and not draw attention to herself, had been momentarily forgotten.

Watching from the top of one of the booths, Wren wanted to fly down and peck out one of the raven's eyes. *What an idiot. Didn't that girl get the message? Was she worth saving when she was so careless with her own safety? If they rescued her, would it be worth it? If she was that stupid, she could get them all killed.*

Wren flew after the raven, knowing that eventually it would have to turn back into its true form. No one could hold another form for too long, especially the shapeshifters who could be anyone. Wren thought it was probably that their bodies needed to recharge more often. She suspected that the girl would turn back to herself to eat her lunch because she thought no one was watching.

Which, again, was stupid. It was the middle of the day. The Preacher was coming to the marketplace in a few hours. His spies could be anywhere.

Wren followed the raven as it flew back to Lopel and into the woods that bordered the beaches. *At least she is smart enough to hide when she changes back and forth,* Wren thought to herself. Wren's patience was rewarded when the raven put the food down on a stump and then transformed into a young woman. Now Wren had the information she might need in the future. She knew what the woman really looked like, not the slightly altered form she showed in public. Wren flew further into the woods before shifting back to being a young woman. She was always careful not to let everyone see how much older she was, even though she knew that Roar and Ruth had found out, and they didn't seem to mind. Still, it was better to be safe.

Wren wondered if she would have to look older when she dealt with the newcomer. It was doubtful that she was used to following rules. But if the newcomer wanted to survive and work with them, she would have to. Otherwise, she would be on her own. And no one would make it on their own with the Kai-Via around.

Seven

Tarek stood in the meadow, enjoying the feel of the wind from the sea as it whipped his cloak behind him, making him look as if he was going to take off and fly. He lifted his face to the sun, enjoying the increasing warmth of Trin as it rose higher in the sky. Thamon's first sun, Etar, was climbing too. It was almost time for the two of them to pass each other in the clear blue sky. It would be a good day to watch the crossing.

Etar didn't give off warmth, it was too far away, and its light was only evident before Trin rose in the morning. But when the two suns passed each other, there were a few moments of something spectacular. The blended lights turned everything a slightly different color, including people. It was a color no one could describe, or reproduce, but everything would look radiant and fresh, if only for that moment.

It was Tarek's favorite time of the day, and he always tried to be outside when it happened. Sometimes there would be a flash of blue at the exact moment of their crossing, and Tarek knew that the people of Thamon had always considered it a good omen for the day.

Or they did. Now that was considered a form of superstition, something banned by the one true religion of Aaron-Lem. Tarek was very familiar with the tenets of Aaron-Lem, and he hated every single one of them. They were easy to hate. And easy to know what Aaron-Lem stood for behind its facade of religion and worship. It was all about ultimate power for one man. Not a god, even though he considered himself to be one. Tarek also knew what happened to nations when they resisted Aaron-Lem.

Tarek was away on a trade ship when his home town was burned to the ground by Aaron-Lem's followers. He returned home to nothing. His home, his family, and his friends were all gone. They had resisted the decree that Aaron was the one true God, and there was to be no more magic or superstitious nonsense lived or even spoken.

Tarek had stood in the middle of the burned town and screamed at that God until the captain of the ship found him and hustled him back to the boat. The captain had kept him sedated until they were safe in open waters. Then he allowed Tarek to stand on the deck and scream until he was exhausted. The rest of the men had stayed silent.

After seeing what had happened to Tarek's homeland, they had quickly replenished the ship's supplies and left, determined to stay as far away as possible from the upheaval that was taking place over all of Thamon.

But Tarek remained angry. If he allowed himself to, he could even now smell the fire and the leftover stench from the burned bodies that had been trapped in their homes and places of business. Tarek couldn't allow himself to return to that memory for long because it drained him of all hope. And he needed that hope, along with his anger.

No matter what it cost him, Tarek was determined to find a way to stop what was happening on Thamon even though he was only one man.

His friends on the ship wanted to stay away, and he couldn't blame them. But he couldn't sit by and watch it happen. So when his ship landed on the shores of Lopel to replenish their supplies, he stayed behind. If there was one place left on the planet not yet entirely ruled by a God who wanted everything his way, he was going to fight to keep it free. And the Islands were that place.

It had been a month since he arrived, all the time staying out of sight while trying to gather all the information that he could about the Kai-Via's methods.

Things appeared different here. Because, so far, it looked as if the Preacher was determined to convince the people through words, not violence, and Tarek was grateful for that fact. Otherwise, more people would have already died. Tarek knew that many were missing. But were they dead, or somewhere else? Did they leave on their own, or were they forced? These were questions he needed to answer, but he knew that they might remain a mystery for the time being.

The Kai-Via was already on the sister island of Hetale, trying to take it over. Lopel was still free enough that he might find a way to stop Aaron's insatiable quest to rule everyone his way. Because Tarek was clear about what was going on.

The religion of Aaron-Lem was not real. Although the message appeared to be about faith, and holiness, it was not. Aaron and his followers had found a way to bend people's minds and make them do what he wanted them to do. Aaron was willing to do whatever it took to be worshiped as the one true God. Anything.

Tarek was willing to do anything to stop him. But he needed help. Finding it had proved more difficult than he thought it would be. Lopel was sparsely populated. Large swaths of meadows and forests took over much of the island. The wind would sweep up and over the white cliffs twisting the limbs of trees in its path into beautiful sculptures, but most people preferred a more sheltered environment. So although there were farms outside the town of Woald, most people on Lopel chose to live within Woald's shelter.

However, he believed that somewhere there were people not seduced by the Preacher's words, and Tarek was determined to find them.

The blue light flashed, and Tarek whooped. It was a good omen. Aaron was afraid of magic because he knew it could defeat his words and his armies. Tarek had to find others who had that magic. He needed help, and it looked as if that help might be in Lopel.

Without giving himself away, he had been observing the wren that followed him. It was careful, staying high in the trees. But birds don't usually move out of their own territories. This one had been tracking him for hours.

Perhaps it was time to show the little bird his true colors. If he was wrong and it was just a bird, so be it. But if he was right, he might have found an ally in his fight against Aaron-Lem.

Eight

Ibris took the letter handed to him by one of the followers that served Aaron-Lem. They were supposed to see to his needs. He found them annoying, always bowing and scraping. They didn't fool him. They weren't bowing and scraping because they thought he was someone worth bowing to. No, they were doing it out of fear.

He grunted to himself, thinking about fear. The people of Hetale hadn't tasted fear. Maybe they should bow to him for keeping blood and destruction from their shores. Then they would know genuine fear. He knew it. He knew what fear felt like. It followed him.

Standing by the sea that morning, he had a moment of release from the pressures and fears that drove him daily. Later, after he had finished his first sermon, he had stepped into the private garden outside his room in the Temple, seeking more relief from what he had to do.

As he sat on the stone bench watching the trees sway in the sea breeze, the blue light flashed, and he hid his smile. His family believed in the omens, and he did too, but he could never let Stryker learn that. It wouldn't matter to Stryker that he was the Preacher that used words better than anyone else on

Thamon. Stryker would simply train someone else, and dispose of him.

The fact that his and the Kai-Via's hooded black robes hid every detail of their bodies and most of their faces was intentional. It allowed them to circulate among the people and watch for unbelievers or rebels. However, there was another reason. They could be replaced if they disagreed with Aaron-Lem or Stryker's methods.

It was close to a miracle that Stryker had given him a season to convert the people without bloodshed. Ibris had nightmares about the destruction they had left behind everywhere else. Why couldn't they have left these Islands alone? What harm would it have done? The rest of Thamon had fallen to Aaron's rule, how could just two small islands isolated far out to sea affect anything else going on?

Ibris mentally shook his head, being careful to never let on what he was thinking or feeling. He couldn't let on that he knew why. He knew that Stryker had plans that Aaron didn't know about.

Thanking the messenger for the letter, Ibris slipped it into the pocket of his robe and stepped back out into his garden. He knew it was from Stryker. It had his seal on it. Black wax, stamped with a coiled snake in the shape of an S. He would open it later because it probably wouldn't be good news, and he needed to prepare for his talk at the market. Sitting in his garden, Ibris calmed his mind and ran through the words he was going to say.

Most of the words wouldn't be heard. Instead, the words would seep underneath what the people expected to hear and slide into their minds. Slowly they would bend to his will, not knowing that was what they were doing. Instead of thinking for themselves, they would soon agree with everything he said.

He was doing them a favor. Every time he spoke to them, he was telling them to surrender. He was telling them to obey the laws and rules of Aaron-Lem. He was telling them that magic was evil and never to be practiced or spoken of. He led them down the dark tunnels of nightmares of what would happen if they practiced magic of any kind. All independent thought was forbidden. They could be happy, raise families, and have normal lives, as long as they followed Aaron, and only Aaron, as their God.

Ibris knew what would happen if they disobeyed, so he worked hard to control them. He wasn't sure that he could handle more blood on his hands. This way was better. He controlled them. He wondered what would happen if Stryker understood that he did it for them, and not for Aaron.

No matter. Stryker would never find out. However, he worried that Dax, the head of the Seven, was beginning to wonder. Dax was a warrior. He wanted to fight. He had been the captain of one of the many armies that Aaron controlled. Troops that moved through countrysides like locusts obliterating everyone who didn't conform.

Dax had been pulled off the front lines by Stryker and transferred to this group of Kai-Via. Ibris knew Dax rankled under this new assignment. Especially since Ibris had been permitted to use conversation instead of bloodshed to bring these remaining Islands into submission.

Ibris suspected that Dax had been placed on the Islands to keep him and the rest of Kai-Via in a constant state of fear. And as much as he tried to control that fear, it was always there, because Ibris could not use words to control Dax.

No matter how skilled he had become using words against others, he couldn't get through to the Seven, especially Dax. He hadn't even tried with Stryker.

All of them had learned how to shut their minds down to suggestions of all kinds against Aaron-Lem. But still, he should have been able to find an opening somewhere. However, so far he had been unsuccessful. Which meant he was going to have to outsmart them all before they discovered that in his heart he wasn't one of them.

He could see with his own eyes that both Aaron and Stryker were just ordinary men, not gods. To Ibris, that was what made them so evil. They claimed to be Ordinary, and they hated anyone with magical skills, no matter how small. They especially hated the shapeshifters who could be anyone. They were not controllable, and that was terrifying to both Aaron and Stryker.

To be sure there were no Mages in his organization, Aaron tested everyone. Including the Kai-Via and Preachers.

Ibris had passed the test using every skill that he had. At the time he felt that he owed his life to Stryker. To please him, he had volunteered to serve in Aaron's organization. Throughout the years he had risen in the ranks. Stryker trusted him. He was tested over and over again and proved his loyalty.

And now he was the most effective of Aaron's Preachers, which made him a very powerful man in Aaron's organization. Powerful enough to request a peaceful conversion for the Islands. But if he failed, Ibris knew there were worse people in Aaron's organization than the armies and the Kai-Via.

If he and the people of Lopel and Hetale were to stay alive, he needed to convert the Islands before the warm months were over, and he would need every one of his skills to do it.

Nine

The Preacher's talk was to be held in the center of the Market. The hope was that people from both islands would be there. Although all of their conversion focus was on Hetale, that was temporary. As soon as they reached a tipping point of conversions on Hetale, they would move on to Lopel. It would be easier because the people of Hetale would have started the process with their friends and relatives.

During high storms seawater would wash over the Arrow, so there were no trees or large plants anywhere on it. Small shrubs that tolerated saltwater and had learned how to survive the rush of waves clung to its sloping sides and along the roadway that existed only because so many carts and people used it every day. Even when the road washed away, it would be back again within days, the earth packed down from centuries of traffic.

Tents of all sizes, shapes, and colors lined the walkway. Each Island favored different colors, so usually it was easy to tell which Island was represented by the booths inside. Lopel favored shades of blue and green, and Hetale liked purple blends with yellow. Sometimes the tents had all those colors because the owners were a combined family. Ibris thought that if he were a bird, the Arrow would resemble a rainbow lying on the ground instead of gracing the skies.

Workers had already erected the Aaron-Lem tent. It took up at least ten tent spaces, and Ibris hoped that his men had been kind and gentle when they displaced the tents that had been there. He would have to assign one of the Seven to make sure the people were giving them the spaces because they wanted to, not because they were forced to. Of course, it was semantics, because Aaron-Lem was always taking. But depending on what words they used, it felt different to the people. For Ibris, it would mean the difference between warfare or an easy conversion. But he knew that men like Dax wanted war.

The Aaron-Lem tent blended all the colors of Hetale and Lopel to imply that they were part of the community. Actually, the intention was to *be* the community, but that was semantics again. Words controlled thoughts, and Ibris needed to be in control of his own first because he was more than afraid; he was nervous. That was not unusual, He always had a case of nerves before speaking. But this time the fear was making it worse. His skill was legendary, but not everyone believed in his mission, and the letter burned a hole in his robe. He was afraid that it meant the Stryker was coming to the Islands to see how he was doing.

What would Stryker see? Would he be pleased with the conversions that they had completed so far? As Ibris walked the roadway to the tent, flanked by the Seven, he looked into the faces of the people lining the way. Which ones were now believers? Which ones were curious? Were there any here who were immune to his words?

Because this was the first talk he would do openly at the Market, there was the chance that there were people in the audience who had heard what they were doing in Hetale and were opposed to it. Unlike the Mages of Hetale who had not been prepared for the takeover, any Mages in Lopel would already be wary.

Dax had insisted that it would be best to get rid of all Mages and shapeshifters as soon as they found them. Ibris was dead set against that tactic. Sooner or later it would be noticed and would put the rest of them on alert. They would hide what they could do. And without a doubt, some of them would form a rebellion.

Of course, that was what Dax wanted. A rebellion. Then he could prove that conversion could not be peaceful. The only power Ibris had in this situation was to keep as many of the Mages and shapeshifters alive as possible in the prison camp on Hetale. If you could call drugged into oblivion alive. But they couldn't take any chances that one of them would regain their strength.

Still, Ibris knew that Dax and his cronies would find a way to eliminate them for good, and he didn't yet have any idea how it could be otherwise. All he could do for now was stall the inevitable and hope that a solution would present itself before it was too late. And keep Stryker on his side, instead of Dax's.

Behind him, Ibris could feel Dax drilling holes of hate into his back. Dax's strength was all physical. He could never be the Preacher. He could not manipulate with words. But he did have the ability to block them, so Ibris didn't try reaching Dax's mind. He concentrated on keeping his own mind from reacting to Dax's subtle taunts, not letting him drag him out of where he had control, and into the pit of Dax's hate.

Turning away from all thoughts of failure, Ibris spread his words out over the crowd, gathering them into the fold of compliance to Aaron-Lem. Even before he stood in front of the crowd that had followed him and now stood watching and listening, he was speaking to them. He told them of the love that Aaron had for them and of the safety they would find by agreeing that Aaron was the one true God.

Once he had them in his spell, he began to explore individual minds, looking for those that were closed to him, or unresponsive.

Sometimes their minds were closed because they were not susceptible to what he was doing, and he would have to change his tactics. Others were doing it on purpose. That made them dangerous. They knew how to block him, and others like him, out of their thinking.

They could hide in the appearance of compliance, but they wouldn't be. And if they were opposed to him and Aaron-Lem they were probably planning a rebellion, and that made them his enemies.

Ten

Meg stood on the outskirts of the crowd and listened to the Preacher. Before coming back to the Market, she had adjusted herself to fit into the crowd, becoming an average Islander. Doing nothing that made her stand out. Meg wore a hat that she had snagged from one of the booths and left her gray cloak hanging on the back of someone's chair. It was too warm out to wear it, and someone might have wondered why she had it on.

If she had a safe place to stay she could keep things there that she needed, but she didn't. At least for now, she was living on the run, and stealing or borrowing was the only way to survive.

Not that Meg was complaining. She liked the freedom of it. She loved being whatever she wanted to be, taking what she wanted to take. Yes, there was a moment of uncomfortableness in the transition from one form to the next, but it was never enough to keep her from changing as often as she wanted to.

She was also one of those shapeshifters who didn't lose their clothes as she shifted from one thing to another. Meg thought it was perhaps a form of memory. The universe remembered and provided it again each time.

Her true, or original, form was not that much different than what she presented most of the time. The changes she made were just subtle enough that no one would notice she was doing it. But transitioning back to her original form was something she never let anyone see. It felt as if she would be giving away some of her magical skills. So, other than her parents and sister, she believed that no one knew what she really looked like.

Everyone in the crowd was talking together, waiting for the event to begin. And then suddenly the crowd went quiet. Meg didn't see any reason for that to happen. No one had said anything or raised a hand to stop the chatter.

There was a long pause as everyone turned to the platform as the Preacher walked to the edge and stood there looking out at the gathering of people waiting for him. Meg watched as he grabbed the crowd's attention and held it.

She was amazed that he was controlling the crowd so effectively even though it was impossible to see what he looked like. He and the Seven behind him wore long black cloaks with a hood pulled over their faces hiding their features in the shadows.

She thought it was incongruous that they were in black when they stood under a multicolored tent. As soon as she thought that, she heard words in her head explaining it.

"It is because we are insignificant. It is the teaching that is important. The colors tell of the joy you will feel as you embrace the one true religion of Aaron-Lem."

She found herself nodding in agreement. Of course, that was why they wore black. It was a perfectly good reason.

A few seconds later, she jerked back in shock, causing someone in the crowd to turn and look at her. Meg quickly composed herself and settled in as if nothing had happened, that it wasn't strange that a voice in her head gave her the answer to something she was wondering about.

The voice came again, soothing her confusion, and reminding her how lovely it was that someone knew what she needed and immediately provided it for her.

This time she let the voice continue to calm her, while carefully closing her mind to any more thoughts going out or coming in. She was very careful. She couldn't let anyone know that she had figured out what was happening. She had to leave a small piece of her thought open so she would appear to anyone searching the minds of the crowd that she was in complete compliance.

In another corner of her mind, she was terrified at what had just happened. Now she knew why the crowd was so happy. Why it felt as if she had stepped into a warm bath of water, floating without any cares in the world. The Preacher was doing it. Somehow he was projecting into each person what they needed to hear to become part of Aaron-Lem.

What had she gotten herself into? She had thought that whoever was stopping Mages was someone she could deal with, if only she had a little help. Or she could go somewhere else, where the Kai-Via and Aaron-Lem did not exist. Now she wasn't so sure.

She stood still with her mind open enough to blend in until the Preacher bowed, stepped down into the crowd, and began walking back to Hetale with the Seven surrounding him, keeping the hands of the people from touching him.

His head was bowed, his hands tucked into the wide sleeves of his robe. Meg moved back through the crowd trying not to draw attention to herself, keeping her mind still, her face placid. She had a feeling if she were too near to him, he would know. The Preacher was not a man to take lightly. Whoever he was, he was in control.

One of the Seven turned to look at the crowd, and only

a quick turn of her head kept him from connecting with her. She had a momentary glimpse of a set of eyes so dark that they appeared black.

Yes, the Preacher was in control, but that one has the fire within him, Meg thought. She didn't think that he cared much about controlling people peacefully. She had a feeling he was all about destroying them.

Eleven

After the Preacher and the Seven were gone, it still took a long time before Meg felt safe again. Her heart had been beating so fast she was afraid she would not be able to stop herself from turning into a raven.

That was something that had happened once before when she was stressed and worried. Before it had been merely embarrassing. If it happened now, it would be dangerous.

The thought of it made her even more afraid, so she made her way as quickly as possible through the crowd that insisted on standing around in a daze. She had the fleeting thought that at least they looked happy.

Once she was clear of the crowd, Meg moved as quickly as possible up the Arrow to Lopel, heading for the town of Woald and the building where she would spend the night. She swept past a booth, leaving her hat and picking up a dark gray cloak displayed on a rack.

Meg was so quick she knew no one saw her, yet it always worried her. But what was she to do? She would need a cloak to ward off the chill tonight, and the hood hid her face.

The Arrow's road extended straight into Woald. Once there, it branched out into all directions. To Meg, Woald felt like a place that grew as needed with no real planning. When new houses were required, a road was made to it, and then other homes and more streets would follow.

Meg had lost count of how many times she had gotten lost the first few days in Woald. But after days of mapping it in her head, she had a good idea of how to get from one place to another.

She took the first right, and then wound her way through the streets, never going straight towards her destination, veering here and there, taking her time. Along the way, she picked up food for the long night ahead. Once Trin set, she used Etar's blue light to find her way to the building, trying to be discreet as she checked behind her to make sure that no one was following her.

Once she thought she saw a cat leap between buildings, but Meg had seen countless cats on the way, so she thought nothing of it, other than that it startled her. She felt like stopping and giving it a tongue lashing, assuming it was still there, but what good would that do? She couldn't take out her fear and frustration on a cat.

Etar was just slipping below the trees in the distance when Meg reached her destination. Checking one last time to make sure she wasn't being watched, she turned the doorknob, sighed because she was finally safe, stepped into the building, and closed the door behind her.

The building was old and dirty, but she had cleaned out one of the rooms and had made a bed of sorts from some blankets she had "found" hanging out to air behind one of the houses in town.

She liked that room. It had a door she could lock and no windows. It felt safe. Her heart had stopped beating so fast now that the scare was over. Too tired to eat, she thought a good night's sleep was just what she needed. Perhaps she would have better luck in the morning finding others like her.

There were no lights in the building, and now that Trin had set there was no light outside either. Thamon didn't have any moons, which felt odd to Meg, but then so did many things in Thamon.

As she stood by the door, waiting for her night vision to kick in, Meg began to feel as if someone else was in the space with her. Too dark to see, she could only hope that she was overreacting.

But when a light flared, she screamed and tried to hide behind some boxes left behind the front door. If it weren't nighttime, she would have transformed into something that could fly or scurry away or even something terrifying like a bear. But she couldn't.

Wren watched Meg cringe and not transform into anything. "Well, well," she said out loud. "This is a problem, isn't it?"

Holding the light, Wren walked over to where Meg was trying to hide and held out her hand to help her up.

"Come on. Let's talk."

Meg just stared at her willing some kind of magic to return if only for a moment, but nothing happened.

"Who are you?" she asked, trying to sound like the powerful shapeshifter she usually was. But it didn't ring true, and besides it was a very young woman who was reaching out her hand. How dangerous could that be?

"It could be very dangerous," another voice said from the darkness, "but luckily for you, we are here to help."

Wren gave up trying to help Meg off the floor and walked over to a table set in the middle of the room. Taking a seat, she placed the light in the center of the table and gestured for Meg to join her.

"You can sit on the floor as long as you feel like, however, sooner or later you are going to have to talk to us. Besides, I think we may be your only hope here on Thamon."

Two other people moved out of the shadows and sat at the table, leaving an open space for Meg.

Cautiously, Meg stepped over to the table and sat down. She saw a young woman, an older woman, and a man—all staring at her as if they knew her.

The young woman said, "Yes, we've seen you before, and you've seen us. But we looked like this."

Meg gasped when seconds later the three old men that had warned her, were sitting at the table. Shapeshifters. The help she needed had come to her.

Twelve

It was time to read the letter.

Everyone had gone, including Dax. But not before he had made his displeasure known. Dax was careful to never openly disrespect Ibris. Instead, he came to congratulate him on how many people had asked to be in the conversion ceremony that took place once a week. The next one would be in two days, and already they had more people than ever before participating.

The ceremonies were a brilliant marketing ploy. At least that was how Ibris saw them. Every service was full of rituals that tugged on the heartstrings of both the participants and the onlookers. Onlookers were encouraged. Family and friends watching the ceremony drove more conversions. It was going so well that soon they would have to increase the number of services held each week.

Dax took Ibris' hand, bowed, and asked if there was anything he could do to help prepare for the ceremony, knowing full well that Ibris had already done everything.

Dax praised Ibris for his ability to hold the crowd with his words, and transform the Islands peacefully. He gushed about how peaceful conversions had never been possible before. Only Ibris' skill was able to pull this off.

If Ibris was less aware, he might have been drawn into Dax's praise. But while Dax spoke, Ibris could feel Dax push into his mind trying to get past the closed door.

Ibris could hear Dax speaking the words that every Preacher always used as they began their sermon, as he tried to open the door into Ibris' mind and control it. Even when the words were not spoken out loud, they were powerful. And Dax was relentless, throwing them again and again into Ibris' mind.

What made it especially galling was Dax knew perfectly well that Ibris could feel the attack, but couldn't acknowledge it. He had no proof. He couldn't go to Stryker and tell him. Dax was Stryker's man. The fight against Dax was his and his alone.

Smirking, Dax left, and Ibris was finally alone. He took the letter out of his robe and headed into the garden. This time, instead of the stone bench, Ibris chose his favorite chair. He had placed it directly under the spreading branches of the Stonenut tree, so named because the shell of the nuts that it produced in the early cold months was as hard as stones.

He imagined that the tree favored him sitting there and gave him strength and wisdom.

But those thoughts had to remain hidden from view. Believing in a power that could be bestowed on people by any of the forms of nature was considered a sin against the authority of the one true God, whose name was Aaron. Giving nature power spoke of superstition and magic, both of which were not allowed anywhere within the doctrines of Aaron-Lem.

Ibris was not a traitor to Aaron-Lem, as much as a disbeliever in its doctrines. But the one doctrine that he did agree with overrode anything else that he might have had a problem with. He believed wholeheartedly in the plan to bring harmony, and happiness, to every person living in Thamon.

Sometimes that meant he had to go to war against anyone

who openly rebelled against Aaron-Lem. Ibris hated doing it, but he believed in the outcome. However, if he could convert the people without harm to anyone except those who openly opposed it, he would rest easier at night.

Ibris cracked open Stryker's seal that was holding the letter closed, the wax peeling away, leaving behind only the faintest mark of the snake on the stark white envelope.

The only words on the front of the envelope were his name, Ibris Elton. Just seeing his full name gave him chills. Elton was his father's name. Ibris had taken it as his last name after his whole family perished in an explosion that obliterated his home town of Oreth.

He shook his head. This was not the time to be thinking of the past. He had to concentrate on what was happening now if he was going to avoid any more bloodshed. Stryker's words were brief, and as Ibris feared, Stryker would be visiting the Islands within the next week.

Stryker expected Hetale to be at least seventy-five percent converted by then if he was going to consider continuing to let the timeline play out for the peaceful conversion of both islands.

Ibris leaned back in his chair and watched the clouds drift by overhead. He was exhausted, and he still had one more sermon to deliver in the Temple that day. Thankfully the evening service was brief, but he knew a day of holding all those minds in his power would send him into a night of pain.

It was the price he paid, and he was willing to pay it. But his time was running out, and he was sure that there was someone in the crowd who had intentionally blocked him while he spoke at the Market.

For a moment he had caught a glimpse of her mind. Before she knew what he was doing and had then carefully stopped his words. He was sure it was a woman. He would have to find her and anyone working with her before Stryker arrived because if Stryker sensed someone like that out there, his response would be typically brutal.

A butterfly landed on a fat yellow flower, not far from where his arm rested on the chair. He turned his head to watch its wings open and close. Closed they were a plain light pink. Open they revealed an intricate design laid out against a darker pink.

He watched the butterfly wings open and shut until his eyes closed, and he let himself imagine himself back home, watching his young sister, Rose, try on her new dress, a light pink dress. His sister, as beautiful as the open wings of the butterfly. Gone, except in his imagination.

Thirteen

"Where are we going?" Meg asked Wren. There was no point in asking anyone else. Wren would have been the one to answer anyway. Meg couldn't keep the irritation out of her voice. *Why was she following this little slip of a person? How old was she anyway?* It wasn't just this one thing that was making Meg irritable. This was not her way.

She was not a rule follower, let alone a person follower. Shapeshifter or not, it didn't make any difference. If she was going to follow the rules, she could have stayed in the Erda dimension and let her parents, and even her older sister, boss her around.

That's why she had run away. To get away from rules. And now she was not only following the rules of a person not much older than a child, but she was also living on a god-forsaken planet that was all about rules. Rules that denied freedom to anyone like her.

Well, there was no real freedom for everyone, but Meg was not used to worrying about other people's freedom. It had only ever been hers that concerned her.

Wren turned and gave her a look that Meg recognized, but didn't want to honor. And yet she had to. If she didn't stay with these three, she was doomed, and at least she was smart enough to recognize that. They understood what that Preacher was doing and how to avoid him and the Kai-Via. If they could get her off the planet, she would happily go home. Yes, she would abandon them. This wasn't her fight.

But at the moment there wasn't a choice. Meg had no idea how to find anyone who knew how to make portals, and no one knew where Meg had come from. The zonking portal maker had done a great job of sending her to what she now realized was what he had hoped to be her death. She would show him. Someday.

In the meantime, she tried swallowing her pride and followed the three to wherever the ziffer they were going. Since it was daylight, she was back to being able to shapeshift again, so she was flying as the raven and Wren was a wren, which made Meg snort in derision when she first saw her. *How typical*, she had thought, but was silenced by a look from all three of them.

The man named Roar was a cat. Seriously? Another stupid name. He obviously wanted to be a lion, but only managed to be a ragged fluffy looking yellow house cat. Or in this case, a feral cat. Birds and a cat. *So stupid*, Meg thought to herself.

Ruth was something else. *Why wasn't she the leader?* Ruth turned into what Meg thought looked like a red fox. *Nice*. Now the four of them were making their way through the woods together. It was like a fairy tale. A wren, a raven, a cat and a fox went into the woods. Meg snorted again to herself. Yes. It was ridiculous, but she still didn't have a choice. For now.

Meg had been full of questions last night, and the three of them answered a few of them. Why not turn into something like a dragon? She came from a family of shapeshifter dragons, and it seemed an easier way to travel.

Wren had turned to her and said, "Well, good thing you

didn't do that. Within minutes you would have been shot out of the sky by the people that serve the Kai-Via and Aaron-Lem. Anything that looks that much like magic is killed immediately, no questions asked."

Wren paused and looked at Meg through squinted hazel eyes, "At least you were smart enough not to do something that stupid."

There had been a moment of tense silence as Roar and Ruth waited to see what Meg would do next. As Meg breathed in, all three of them had silently prepared their defenses. But wisely Meg had stopped herself. So far these three were the only other Mages of any kind that she had found. And they were organized. Meg knew herself well enough to know that organization was not her strong suit.

In the back of her mind, she wondered what her strong suit was? Other than doing whatever she wanted to do when she wanted to do it. No mission, no plan, nothing but fun. On Thamon, having fun did not look like a wise survival technique.

Meg never got an answer from anyone about where they were going. So she followed Wren as they flew to the far end of Lopel. It wasn't a big island. Someone could probably walk the circumference of the island in a day. Woald was the only city or town. The people who lived away from Woald were mostly farmers. And even then, they often lived in Woald and then went to work in the farms during the day, leaving one or two members of their family at the farm overnight.

Below them, Meg could see the farmhouses with plumes of smoke rising from chimneys in both the barns and homes. Burning off the morning chill or perhaps cooking, she thought. Meg could also see what looked like horses and cows.

From this far away, they looked very similar to the ones she knew from home. If she was smarter, perhaps she could figure out how that happened. How did people and animals so like the ones at home on the planet Gaia come to be on Thamon? At the moment that wasn't a survival question, so she would wait to ask it another time.

Last night Meg had learned that the three were actually from the other island, Hetale. But Hetale was rapidly falling under the spell of the Preacher and Aaron-Lem, so they decided to switch their meetings to Lopel. Hetale was a slightly smaller island, which may be why the Kai-Via had chosen to begin its conversions there. *It was as good a reason as any,* Meg thought.

Wren dipped her wings and flew down to the forest floor, and Meg followed. Roar and Ruth were not far behind, and all four turned back into their original form as they arrived, conserving energy. *Were they that safe?* Meg wondered. She looked around and saw nothing other than a forest, just like the one that was outside Woald. What were they doing here?

A second later, there was a flash of light, and standing before them was a man wearing a cloak and carrying a staff—the universal sign of a wizard. Wren laughed, "Good show, Tarek. The staff is a nice touch."

The man called Tarek smiled and bowed to Wren. "I thought you would like that, child."

Instead of bristling, Wren beamed, and Meg stared at her in shock. What was going on here?

Turning to look at Meg, the man Wren called Tarek asked, "And who do we have here?"

Fourteen

Meg just stood there and stared. It was Wren who answered, "She is a newcomer to Thamon. We rescued her."

"What?" Meg exploded, "You didn't rescue me. I was doing just fine without you."

Wren, Roar, and Ruth started laughing. "Zut, you are easy to provoke," Wren said. "And yes, we did, because with that temper and your lack of awareness it wouldn't be long before the Kai-Via found you.

"The Preacher saw you for a moment. Now he will be looking because now he knows you exist."

Meg glared at the four of them and then turned her back to hide her face. She didn't know if she was angry or sad. Probably both. Wren spoke the truth, but that didn't mean she had to like it. But now that she had turned away, how was she going to save face and turn back around?

What a mess I am making of things, Meg thought.

It was the man called Tarek that saved her pride. He started talking as if nothing had happened. "Well, I am delighted we have another member of our little group. But let's not just stand here. I have someplace we can talk that will be safer. You never know who is watching."

Even Meg looked around at that statement. If someone were watching, they would have to be a practitioner of some form of magic, and probably a shapeshifter. Why would they be against them? But since there were no answers to that question, she stoically turned and followed Tarek as he led them through the trees. A few minutes later, they were standing on the edge of a small cliff. Looking down, they could see a mass of flat stones in front of what looked like an opening in the earth.

"A cave?" Meg asked. "Are we going in there?"

"Yes, a cave, and yes, we are going in there. I made us a boat."

It was only then that Meg noticed water lapping against the opening. It was dark. Wet. Closed in. She started shaking. Everyone pretended not to notice. Reluctantly Meg followed Tarek as he led them to the side of the cliff where simple steps were carved into the hillside.

"No, I didn't make the steps," Tarek said. "I discovered them under the overgrowth. They must have been here a long time, but no one seems to have used them for many years."

Meg wished they weren't using them now, but there was nothing to do but follow the other four down. Perhaps it wouldn't be as bad as it looked. At first, it was. Actually, it was worse. The boat was rocking, water lapped over the side, and the cave was dark and cold. She could feel a cold wind coming from the cave as if it was breathing. Meg's shaking got worse.

Tarek barely glanced at her. Instead, as they passed through the opening into the cave, everything changed. The boat began to glide, a soft light lit up the sides of the cave revealing how beautiful it was, and it felt as if a heater had come on.

Meg was so thankful, tears sprung to her eyes, and she dropped her head so that no one would notice.

She forced a "thank you," out of her mouth, and Tarek smiled and nodded. For the next couple of minutes, he pointed out the many beautiful structures that seemed to have dripped from the ceiling. Sometimes they hung from the ceiling, and other times they grew up from the floor. Drops stacked upon drops. There were ledges along the walls, and Meg thought perhaps people had once walked there, the shelves seemed big enough.

"Yes," Tarek answered her unspoken question. "I believe that at one time, people did live here. But if they did, it was a long time ago.

"I wanted to show you this cave because it will be a safe place to meet and we are going to need it."

Looking at Meg, he added, "And you won't need me to smooth out the waters or light and heat the cave. I set that in motion already for the four of you. For anyone else that is not part of our group, it will remain dark and dangerous."

"How will you know who is part of our group?" Ruth asked. "Aren't we the only ones left who are Mages or shapeshifters?"

"Well, since Wren only found me yesterday, there is no reason there aren't others like you. But for now, it's just the five of us."

"Where did you come from, Tarek?" Roar asked. "Wren just told us that she followed you because she suspected that you were something other than a man walking through the field."

Roar looked over at Wren with an admiring glance. "She's good at that. It's how she found Meg, too. But really, we don't know how the two of you arrived on these islands. Obviously, Meg is a shapeshifter, and you are … what, a wizard? But where did you come from? The three of us know everyone on these Islands, and neither of you were here before."

Tarek laughed and looked over at Meg, "Do you want to go first, or me?"

Meg glanced at the four of them. "It's not a big mystery. I stepped through a portal, and here I am."

"Where were you before, and why did you come here?" Ruth

asked.

"I'm from Erda, one of the dimensions on the planet Gaia. I didn't come here on purpose. I asked a portal maker to send me someplace where I could be free."

Wren started laughing so hard she snorted, and the boat began rocking and taking on water. Meg glared at her as Wren said, "I guess that portal maker didn't like you much."

"Obviously," Meg answered, and then shut her mouth making it clear that was all she was going to say.

All eyes turned to Tarek and never left him as he told the story of a burned-out homeland, a planet entirely overrun by Aaron-Lem, and how he arrived on a trading ship, stayed, and why.

Wren bowed her head, as the other three took in what Tarek was telling them. They were in so much more trouble than they had thought. How were they going to stop the religion from destroying all magic, and the freedom to be anyone they wanted to be?

"It gets worse," Tarek said. "Stryker is on his way to the Islands."

Looking at the other four, Tarek realized no one knew who Stryker was, but once he told them they would be even more afraid.

Still, in spite of their fear and the smallness of their numbers, they were going to stop the Preacher, Stryker, and finally Aaron. He was determined.

He would make it so or die trying, and he had no intention of dying.

Fifteen

"So do you have a plan?" Meg asked Tarek after he told them about Stryker. She wasn't sure she liked Tarek yet. Not that it mattered whether she liked him or not. But having been betrayed by the portal maker, she was now worried that she had no sense of who was lying to her or not.

"Do you?" was Tarek's counter.

"I just got here," Meg snapped.

"And so did I," Tarek shot back.

Meg and Tarek glared at each other until Wren huffed and stomped her foot. "And this is why I have been the leader."

Tarek laughed and hugged Wren, "And you have been doing a zonking good job of it, too. You found the two of us. Have you found any more people hiding their magical skills that would like to join this band of rebels?"

The word rebel woke Meg up. "That's what we are, aren't we? Rebels!"

When everyone stared at her, not understanding her reaction, she added, "That's what I have been my whole life. A rebel. Only I was rebelling just for the thrill of it, and for myself, nothing more than that."

Turning to Tarek, she asked, "Are we really rebels? Is that

what this is about?"

Tarek took in Meg's earnest face and wondered if it was the first time she had ever felt a purpose. "Yes, that's what it is about. We are rebelling against a man who wants to rule the world. You rebelled against rules. That, I think you can now see, was shortsighted. Rules are necessary for people to have guidelines. Ethical rules are like a guardrail along a cliff. They protect you by keeping you from falling over it by mistake.

"However, when rules are put in place so that a person, or a group of people, can control everyone to their advantage then those rules are something to rebel against. Absolute authority is an evil. Anyone with that kind of power eventually begins justifying the elimination of anyone who doesn't agree with them. And that is what has happened in Thamon.

"Aaron says he is the one true God. We all must worship him and the religion he named after himself. He demands absolute authority. Aaron declares that freedom and happiness are found only in his religion, and by following his rules."

"And his rule is that no one can practice magic?" Meg asked.

"More than that. No one can have a magical skill of any kind, practiced or not. Aaron has decided that anyone who rebels against his rules must be a Mage, which gives him the right to have them eliminated under the laws that he made. That means that thousands of regular, or ordinary people, have died along with the Mages.

"Aaron hates the shapeshifters the most not just because they can be anyone, but the symbol that they can be anyone promises a different kind of freedom, even for non-shapeshifters and Mages.

"Aaron claims that you can't be anyone you want to be. You have to be the role that makes you the most useful in society. And he and Stryker determine what that will be."

The five of them sat in the boat, no one saying anything as they thought through what Tarek had said. As they sat together in silence, Meg realized that she wouldn't mind staying in the cave forever. It had become so peaceful. *But then that wouldn't be rebelling against anything, would it?* Minutes went by, each one lost in thought. It became so silent that Meg's head drooped and she found herself falling asleep. She wondered if all the danger had been a dream, and she would wake up soon.

She really thought she was dreaming when she heard, "Shh." Looking up without raising her head, she saw Tarek with a finger on his lips. He pointed towards the mouth of the cave. *What did he see?* Finally, Meg heard a small sound, a rustle, a whoosh, and then saw what looked like a shadow pass in front of the opening.

Surprisingly she felt no fear. *Was it because whatever they were seeing had blocked her from being afraid?* There was no time to figure it out because a split second later a small light flared in front of her face, and then something plopped into the bottom of the boat.

All five of them stared down at what looked like a wet lump of feathers lying at the bottom of the boat. It was blinking on and off.

"What is that?" Wren asked.

"That," Tarek answered, "is an Okan. Her name is Silke Featherpuff. Why that is her name is obvious. What isn't obvious is, what is she doing here? And why is she all wet?"

"That's a fine way to great your friend," the lump of wetness said. "And I misjudged where the water was. Phew, cold!"

By then, the Okan had shaken the water off herself, and Meg could see that it looked more like a tiny person, and what she had thought were feathers was her hair. Very feathery hair.

"Seriously, Silke," Tarek said, staring down at the now almost dry Okan. "I thought I told you to stay on the ship. Thamon is not a safe place for you to be."

"And this is a safe place for you?" Silke countered, hands on her hips, staring right back at Tarek. "My place has always been with you, and I didn't appreciate you trying to leave me behind."

After giving Tarek one last look, Silke turned to look at the other people on the boat. When she got to Meg, she squinted her eyes and said, "And who is that?"

"Meg from Erda," Tarek answered.

Meg turned to Tarek and asked. "Is she here to help or give me dirty looks?"

Wren stood up, causing the boat to sway a bit. "Seriously. This is why I am in charge. Until you can all act like grownups, I will decide what we do. Tarek, thank you for bringing us the information about the larger world, but now we need to deal with what is happening here.

"Let's look at what each of us can do, including Miss Featherpuff here, and start rebelling. Are you all in, or is this a waste of my time?"

Ignoring Silke's reaction at being made fun of, Wren looked around the boat for confirmation. Once she received nods of yes from everyone except Silke who was still pouting, she said, "Okay, Tarek, you must have come here with a plan. What was it?"

Sixteen

The men on the ship did their best not to show their terror. But even a glimpse of the man called Stryker struck fear in their hearts. They would turn to their task, hoping he hadn't noticed their faces, or that they were doing their job the way that he wanted it done. There were stories of what Stryker could, and would do to people that displeased him.

Before boarding the ship, Stryker had assured himself that there were no Mages on board and that every single man had converted to Aaron-Lem. His methods were brutal, and that only fueled their current fear.

Still, Stryker kept a watchful eye out for anyone doing something they weren't supposed to be doing, or not doing what they were assigned to do.

Either way, he would punish them. He couldn't kill them outright or injure them too gravely. Each man was needed to keep the ship functioning. But he could make them feel a world of hurt.

It was his way of keeping control. There were easier ways, but not as visible, and he needed his ways to be visible so that any thoughts of rebellion would have no room to fester. Stryker hated ships. They were so zonking slow. But he had to appear ordinary. Not a Mage. Not a wizard. No use of magic at all. At least in public.

So he couldn't just appear somewhere the way he used to. He even had to pretend that his Falcon was a trained bird. A bird that did his bidding. Delivered his messages. Spied for him. But to others, it was just a bird, nothing more.

Stryker was hungry. Not just for the food he knew his chef was preparing for him, but hungry for his quest to be over, because when it was over, he could throw away his disguise, and return to himself. *Imagine Aaron's surprise when he finds out,* Stryker thought to himself.

He felt movement behind him and instinctively readied himself to strike, his reaction hidden within his long cloak, and in the subtle and barely noticeable focusing of his muscles.

But he relaxed as he smelled the food. The chef had arrived with three servers, two men carrying a table, another with a chair, one with an umbrella to shield him from the sun, and one bringing the plates and silverware. The chef directed the action and then stood ready, hands behind his back, prepared to answer Stryker's questions about the food.

The cook motioned one man forward. He had the honor of tasting every dish. If he didn't fall sick, he was excused with the rest of the men, just as hungry as before, but maybe more so after tasting the food he and the other men on the ship would never have a chance to eat.

When nothing happened to the man, Stryker gestured for all of them to leave him. He sat down, spread his perfectly white napkin on his lap, and settled in to eat enough food to feed all the men who had just stood in his presence for the entire day.

Stryker wouldn't eat it all. What was left, he would toss overboard. Sometimes birds or fish would see the food before it sank into the waves and he enjoyed watching them fight over it.

If Falcon were around, he would allow him to eat from the food on his table before throwing it overboard, but today Falcon wasn't there. He hadn't yet returned from delivering the message to Ibris.

Ibris. Now that was a man worth watching. Yes, he was the most effective Preacher they had ever had. Ibris had taken to the training like a drowning man, needing a purpose to live.

Which of course he did, after everyone he loved had died. Training Ibris was playing with fire. But Stryker didn't mind, he knew how to put out fires, and for the moment he needed Ibris to finish what he started, and then, well, he would see.

Just a few more days and he would be on the islands. It was there Stryker would begin his search for the one thing that would make him all-powerful. With it, even Aaron would not be able to defeat him.

****

Leon, the cook, backed away from Stryker as he began to eat, holding the thought in his mind of the glory of Aaron-Lem. He mumbled the prayer he had learned at the Temple. "Blessed be Aaron, the one true God. Blessed be his holy name."

Every man with him did the same. He had taught them to keep the prayer running at all times while on the ship with Stryker. Leon carefully chose each man to work with him. They had known each other for years, and when Aaron-Lem arrived in their country, they had fled with their families long before the bloody take-over had begun.

For many centuries there had been a prophecy of the Aaron-Lem's coming, and Leon's people had taken it seriously. Generations had gone by, and the preparations seemed as if they had not been necessary. Some of his people had drifted away and forgotten. His friends and his family had not. So when the first signs appeared, signs that had been passed down from generation to generation, he paid attention.

When it was clear that what his ancestors had predicted had arrived on Thamon, he put the generations of preparation into action. Because they accepted the signs, they had time to disappear without anyone questioning what they were doing.

Long before the news of the destruction of the first city, half of them had already arrived in the new land. The rest followed, taking their time, saying they were off to visit relatives, or selling their homes because they were going to go live in a warmer country. They all had different reasons for going, and Leon was sure that no one had questioned why they were leaving.

After making sure their loved ones were safe and secure, Leon asked for volunteers to defeat Aaron-Lem. He picked a handful of them based on their skills, and the remainder stayed behind to protect and care for the others. Eight of them were on the ship with him.

They trained hard to appear to be the empty vessels that Stryker and Aaron demanded of them. They stayed still and silent and waited. Stryker had his food tasted for poison. What he didn't know is that *they* were the poison. Slow, silent, and someday, deadly.

Seventeen

Preparation for the conversion ceremony was in full swing when Wren and her friends returned to Woald. They had stayed an extra day near the cave, getting to know each other better.

As happy as Wren was to add more people to the team, she wasn't sure about the newcomers. She, Roar, and Ruth hadn't known each other that long either. However, they had been working together, and she trusted them. Besides, they listened to her.

That Meg, she was a wild card. But Tarek seemed to have a good handle on how to deal with her. *Perhaps she is trainable, Wren mused.* Tarek had agreed with Wren that they needed to know each other better.

However, Tarek wanted to concentrate on what he considered the most crucial questions: What could they be? What were their skills? One day was not nearly enough to find out all that they needed to know, but it would have to do.

Silke had confirmed that Stryker was due on the island in a few days. He was known for his violent ideas. He would not be happy that Ibris' peaceful takeover seemed to be working, so he would want to find a reason for bloodshed.

The news was disturbing. *What could their small group do to stop it?* Wren wondered. *There were only five of them. Okay six if you counted the Miss Featherpuff thing.*

The question in Wren's mind was why Stryker and the Kai-Via bothered to come to the Islands. They had conquered the rest of the world. What was on the islands that made it so crucial that the Kai-Via needed to convert it, and why did Stryker bother to come himself? Something else was happening. They were obviously missing some critical piece of information.

It was one reason why Wren was watching the conversion ceremony with Roar by her side. They watched the preparation in silence together. Today they looked like a young girl and her father. The two of them blended in perfectly, swaying a bit with the crowd, minds blank except for delight at the preparations.

If Wren hadn't known why the Temple was decorated the way that it was, she might have been delighted with what she was seeing. Long streamers hung from the beams that held up the octagon-shaped Temple.

During the warm months, the walls of the Temple could be rolled up into the ceiling above the rafters, leaving all the walls completely open except for the back wall that faced north. That wall held the altar and the platform where the Preacher stood.

The streamers acted as a partial see-through wall during the ceremony. Those that were being converted were inside the Temple. The onlookers stayed outside, seeing only glimpses of what was going on through the colorful waving streamers. If you wanted to see what happened in there, you had to be part of the ceremony.

The crowd outside stood on a flagstone patio that surrounded most of the Temple. Large branching trees grew along the edges providing shade. If it rained, the people would continue to stand there getting drenched, but not minding.

They accepted that the rain was sent directly from the one

true God to bless them.

Inside the Temple, a massive pool of water had risen from beneath the floor. The water was level with the floor of the Temple so the converts could easily step into the pool. Those who had trouble walking were carried. Because healings had been reported after people stepped into the pool, the rush to get in was intense. The Kai-Via had to monitor how many people came in at one time so that nobody got hurt in the rush to be first.

Once the pool was full, the Preacher appeared on stage. To avoid the appearance of magic, he never just appeared. He was announced. He walked in like an ordinary person. No sleight of hand was allowed in Aaron-Lem. Aaron and Stryker could not take the chance that someone might accuse the Kai-Via of having magic themselves.

The pool was warm and only came to the knees of most of the people. Young children held their parent's hands, and babies' feet were lowered to touch the water.

As the Preacher began the blessing, a hidden chorus chanted. From the ceiling, a mist of scented water descended on all those standing in the pool. Lights danced upward from beneath the water, coloring the faces of the converts and turning the mist into tiny colored jewels.

Murmurs of joy began escaping the mouths of the converts in the pool and spread through the crowd standing outside. Although they could only see a little of what was going on, they could hear the music and catch brief moments of the Preacher's words. In the crowd, many had already gone through the ceremony, and they re-lived what had happened for them. That memory fueled the desire of others to be converted. If it meant that life was always going to feel this good all the time, they wanted to be part of it.

The Preacher's words rose and fell, mesmerizing the crowd. There was no part of the ceremony that had not been carefully crafted to stimulate a positive, emotional response, and trigger a yearning to be part of what was going on.

If you had never experienced the ceremony, you were an outsider. An increasingly lonely outsider as more and more people chose to convert.

The ceremony was Ibris' idea. He wanted to prove to Aaron and Stryker that this kind of manipulation was much more potent than creating fear.

However, even Ibris knew that not all people fell under its spell. He could feel blanks in the crowd where his words did not reach. He knew that he would have to search those people out separately. If they were unintentionally unaffected, then he had another way to reach them. Not as pleasant, but not as terrible as Stryker's method of discarding them. If they were doing it on purpose, he had a choice. He wasn't sure what he would choose.

Ibris used the power of his words to lift himself out of his confusion. He prayed to know that he would have the wisdom and courage to do what he needed to do.

The ceremony ended with a request for a blessing for all that had turned to Aaron and worshiped him. Everyone bowed their head. Ibris caught Dax looking out over the gathering. He knew that his words never got through to Dax. That was the other kind of mind that blocked him, the ones that hated him. Hated him for making peace.

It was a heavy price to pay to have everyone under the spell of his words, to allow them no thoughts of their own outside the doctrine of Aaron-Lem. But it saved their lives. However, no matter what Ibris did to try and stop him, Dax continued to desire the taking of lives. Sooner or later, one or the other of them would win.

Eighteen

After everyone had gone, Tarek and Silke settled in to have the discussion they both knew was coming. They had things to resolve. Tarek wanted to understand why Silke had not obeyed him when he had told her to remain on the ship. That was the conversation he knew he was supposed to have. But, truthfully Tarek was happy to have Silke with him again.

Sometimes she annoyed him to no end, but she was a fierce protector of what was right, and of him. Even as a child, when he got himself into trouble by not obeying the rules, it was Silke who smoothed over what he had done. His parents would listen to what she had to say, and then, for the most part, take her suggestions about how to discipline him.

First, he had to explain to them why he had broken the rules. If he could convince them of the wisdom of his decision, they would thank him for helping them see things a different way. However, if he broke the rules just because it was fun and he liked watching the cascade of consequences, that was a different story.

Then, he was required to help repair any damage he had done to any person, place, or thing, no matter how big or how small. He had learned how easy it was to do something that radically changed someone's outlook on life, or their life itself, just because he was acting out.

It changed the way he looked at the world and the people in it. But mostly it changed the way he saw himself in the world. His parents, with Silke's help, had molded him into what he was today. And that was why he was no longer on the ship, keeping himself safe—staying away from the turmoil going on in the world.

If he had stayed, he would have grieved for the rest of his life over the loss of his family. Grieved or blamed himself because he hadn't been there to save them. There were all the "ifs" of what he could have done differently.

If he hadn't loved the carefree life of a sailor on a trade ship. If he had stayed home and worked the land. If he had been more like his brothers and sisters and stayed rooted to a place. If he had stayed home, he could have kept them safe.

And if he hadn't saved them, at least he could have perished with them, and they would be in that land behind the veil together. All those "ifs." None of which had happened.

Yes, he could have destroyed himself with guilt or sorrow, but he chose something different. Instead, he had chosen to fight. How he knew that the Islands were where the final battle would be fought was another story. One that he knew he would someday have to tell "the rebels," as he now thought of the little group they had. But for now, it was probably for the best that they got to know him better first.

Wren was doing a fantastic job of leading their little group, and he was perfectly happy to step back and let her. With a bit of help from him as needed, of course.

Tarek leaned back against the smooth bark of a Yellowblossom tree and watched Silke play in the meadow. Besides needing to talk things out, they had also stayed behind to give Silke time to rest. The ship had been a few days out to sea before she had managed to escape the room that he had locked her in after telling her that she could not come with him.

Tarek knew she would eventually get out, and the crew would care for her. They loved her as much as he did. He reasoned that she would be too far away to come back to the Islands, and would continue with the ship, safely away from Aaron.

He had no idea she could make that flight across the sea. Now he realized how stupid he had been. She could have died making the trip. But Silke was nothing if not resourceful. She had told him that more than once she had hitched a ride with a bird going her way. Sometimes with their permission, sometimes not. But she always repaid them by directing them to where they would find food for themselves.

But by the time she arrived on Lopel, she was barely functioning, having not eaten for days. Silke told Tarek she had crawled into the forest and fallen asleep on a bed of moss. When she woke, she found mushrooms and feasted on them until she felt better. Of course, being Silke, she had embellished the story. And even though Tarek knew that she was manipulating him to punish him for leaving her, he still found himself in tears as she told of her journey to find him.

The easiest part was finding him after she felt better. All she had to do was follow the invisible thread that tied them together.

"Had you forgotten?" Silke asked, giving him a look of pure sadness. "I can't survive long without you anyway. You snapped the thread when you left me behind. If I hadn't made it to the Islands, I wouldn't have survived on that ship."

Tarek had stared at her in horror. No, he hadn't thought about that. He thought it was a tale told to him to keep in line as he went around breaking the rules. Not for a second had he believed it, or he would never have left her behind.

"'Didn't you feel the thread snap?" Silke had asked.

"Yes, but I thought it was because I felt so keenly the loss of you. But, I knew I could survive it if you were safe," Tarek answered.

The two of them stared at each other for a long time. Silke's inner light blinking on and off in a slow, steady rhythm. During the day, her light was hard to see. At night, she could control the timing of the light and leave it on longer than off. It had been a beacon of safety for all of Tarek's childhood. All he could think to himself was that he was an idiot. Silke didn't disagree with him.

So, they had stayed for Silke to recover, and for Tarek to reevaluate how he chose to do things. For the thousandth time in his life, he readjusted his world view, while below in the meadow, thousands of butterflies took flight. In the middle of the winged flock, Silke rose, swirling and playing. It was so beautiful to see that it brought tears to Tarek's eyes. He still had a family. He had Silke. This time he would not ever forget it.

Nineteen

Stryker opened the map that he kept with him at all times. How many times had he stared at it? He had lost count. It had been his prized possession since the moment he had found it. At least when he was younger, that's what he had thought. That he had found it.

But as he grew older, he became positive that he was the only person in all of Thamon that was supposed to have it.

No one else knew about it. It was his precious secret. Although sometimes Stryker worried that Aaron suspected that there was something on Stryker's mind other than converting the entire planet of Thamon to the one true religion of Aaron-Lem.

Oh yes, he did want to do that. He wanted the whole planet out of their minds. Literally. They would lose the capacity to do any independent thinking. Aaron-Lem's promise of a better, happier, and more fulfilled life was what the Ordinaries wanted. And he and Aaron would provide that for them in return for turning their lives into unutterably non-imaginative lives.

It was ironic that that was what Aaron-Lem produced, since the way they controlled the people was through imagination. Stryker shook his head at the irony of it. He and Aaron had taught all the Preachers the secret, but no one else knew. Not that it mattered that much since there were very few people thinking in Thamon anymore.

His preachers were his prized project. At one time there were almost a hundred of them. Some of the Preachers that he had trained were still preaching for Aaron. Others had proved completely ineffective, so Stryker had eliminated them. A few of the Preachers had turned against him. That hadn't lasted long. They, too, were eliminated.

It bothered Stryker that Ibris was the most effective Preacher he had. Something about Ibris didn't ring true, but Stryker couldn't put his finger on what it was. Ibris was effective. He was obedient. He never tried to control anyone other than the people they were converting.

So for now, Stryker left Ibris in place. Ibris was fulfilling his role with distinction, and that meant the Islands were going to be easy to take over.

And the Islands were the key to everything. It had taken him most of his life to figure out the map. For years he had tried to find out what the landmass was on the map. In school, he had studied all the continents, looking for the same shape that he saw on the map. He couldn't ask for help because then someone else would know what he had.

One day he was in the library and pulled out an atlas of the world that he had never seen before. He opened it at random and almost fell out of his chair. He had let out a whoop of astonishment, and everyone in the library stared at him as if he had gone crazy. Silent Stryker had shown joy. That in itself was astonishing.

But he had ducked his head, and eventually they had stopped looking at him, and he allowed himself to look at the atlas again hoping that what he had seen was real. When all eyes had returned to what they had been doing, he secretly pulled the map out of his pocket—even then he always had it with him—and compared it to the pictures.

Tears of happiness had sprung to his eyes. Finally, he had found the place. It was a beginning. He had discovered the twin islands of Lopel and Hetale, so far away he had never heard of them before.

Next, he had to find out why it was a map of two small islands. Why was the map so vital that it was hidden so carefully? For years. Waiting for him. It was a long time before he discovered what the map had revealed, and now he was close to getting it.

Closing his eyes, Stryker let the rocking of the ship lull him as he thought back to how he first found the map, and what that first look had done to him.

He had only been a child. He had gone outside to play before Trin rose, which he often did. He loved how Etar bathed their backyard in blue light. It was the middle of the warm months, and the trees were fully leafed out. Etar's light filtered through branches and leaves creating strange shadows on the ground.

It was his favorite time of day. It was his private time before all the grownups wanted him for chores and studies. It was the in-between time. Night animals had already returned to their homes, and the day animals had not yet ventured out. A lone bird or two would sing in the forest, but most of them waited until the rising of Trin before beginning the morning chorus.

That morning had been special. It was his birthday. He was seven. His people considered seven a transition age. He was old enough to reason. He would be given more responsibilities after today. But first, today was his day. It was a day of presents, and friends, his favorite foods, and hugs that he endured.

It had seemed to Stryker that the whole world was poised to celebrate with him. The blue light was brighter. The shadows deeper. It was magical. Stryker had loved magic. His mother was an Ordinary, but his father had some magical skills. That morning Stryker had been wondering if he was an Ordinary, or if he had inherited some of his father's abilities. Most people didn't find out until they were at least seven years old, which made this day even more special. It was the promise of what he might discover about himself.

So that day he was looking for magic even more than he usually did, which meant that he wasn't surprised when one of the shadows on the ground morphed into what looked like an arrow. *Ha*, he had thought. *A sign, just for me!*

Without hesitation, he had pointed himself in the direction of the arrow and started walking. He wasn't supposed to go far from home, but Stryker was absolutely certain that he was doing the right thing. Even if his mother didn't understand, his father would.

Once he lost sight of the first arrow, he saw another one. Arrow shadows on the ground. He knew he had to hurry. Once Trin rose, the shadows would disappear. Stryker knew this was a gift he could only receive on this day.

So he ran, stumbling through the forest, branches morphing into arrows until the moment that Trin rose and a bright shaft of sunlight streaked through the forest landing on a large rock sitting in an opening in the trees. This was it. He knew this was where he would find his treasure. But he didn't have time to find it that day. His parents would be frantic with worry. He had a piece of chalk in his pocket, so he knew what to do. His mother always scolded him for leaving chalk in his pocket, but he loved marking things. That day, he marked trees as he made his way home so he could easily find his way back

If it hadn't been his birthday, he would have been in serious trouble for coming home so late in the morning. But since it was his special day, he only got a mild scolding. Stryker wished he could have told his father what he had found, but even then he knew the treasure was only for him. The next morning Stryker found his way back to the rock armed with a shovel. After digging under the rock for over an hour, he found the map that would transform his life.

There had been a price to pay. But he didn't know that until much later, and he wasn't sure that he would have turned it down even if he had known what the price would be. He thought his parents, especially his father, would have understood if he would have known.

Twenty

Meg slipped out of her hiding place in the old building and made her way to the Conversion Ceremony on Hetale. She had come back to the building to rest after the meeting with Tarek and that piece of fluff he called Silke. She hadn't wanted to admit how tiring that whole trek had been.

It wasn't the physical journey to the cave and back that had tired her out. It was what was being asked of her. She was used to being a free spirit. Now, if she wanted to stay alive, she had to play by some rules. Follow the guidance of others. Play nice. It was exhausting.

Meg was self-aware enough to know that most of the exhaustion stemmed from the push and pull going on inside of her. She wanted to run, and she needed to stay. Not just because it was safer with the group, but because something inside of her was beginning to care.

Not enough to keep her from thinking that if she had a chance, she would escape Thamon in a heartbeat, but enough to worry what would happen to others if she left.

If this was what it was like to be part of a group, she could see why she had always chosen to be her own universe, with its own rules. Because there was no one she could tell these thoughts to, she was silent on the way back to Woald.

Wren had told her to go to the building and get some rest, and at first, Meg wanted to snap back at her that she would do what she wanted to do. She stopped herself when, in a rare moment of clarity, she realized that Wren was giving her permission to do exactly what she wanted to do. She didn't have to sneak off and hide or lie about what she was doing.

So she had nodded and walked away from the other three, shifting into a mouse the last few blocks so she could get into her building undetected. She had barely made it into her bed before changing back to her true form and falling asleep.

She dreamed about her sister searching for her. In the dream, Meg wanted Suzanne to find her. When she woke, she wondered if the dream was trying to tell her something.

Not that it mattered whether she wanted Suzanne to find her or not. There was no way. She was on her own. Well, not entirely alone. Now there was Miss Featherpuff and Tarek, and Wren, Roar, and Ruth. If she had met any of them under any other circumstances, she would have never looked their way. *Well,* she thought to herself, *not entirely true. Who wouldn't look Tarek's way?*

Ruth had told Meg to meet her at the Temple. "How will I find you?" Meg had asked Ruth, who answered, "I'll find you."

Meg didn't think so. How would Ruth know what she would look like? But that was Ruth's problem. She would go, hang out and watch whatever this big thing was, and then explore Hetale on her own because that was what was supposed to happen.

She was supposed to get to know Hetale, see if she had any sense as to what happened to the other Mages and shapeshifters that used to live there. What had the Kai-Via done with them?

Meg took her time crossing the Arrow, dressed like all the other women who lived on the Islands, careful to take food when no one was looking, and never too much from the same food stall. The Market was quiet, much of the crowd on their way to watch the ceremony. Meg slipped into the crowd, slowly adjusting herself to look even more as if she belonged.

Tarek had asked her to listen to conversations instead of remaining in her thoughts, so she practiced listening as she walked. At first, everyone talked about the weather, something they had just purchased at the Market, or how they felt. But as they got closer to the Temple, the conversation slowly came to a stop.

It was if a fog had drifted over them and was dulling their thinking. Meg could feel it within herself. Like fog, the dampening effect kept trying to find cracks in her mind to slip into. *Interesting,* she thought to herself. *It was as if the people were being drugged by something.*

Having been at the Preacher's talk, she recognized the same kind of power at work. Then, it had been the Preacher who was telling her what to think. Now, it was the fog that dulled thinking. And made people feel happy, Meg realized, looking at the people around her. They were acting like mindless sheep.

To keep anyone from noticing her, Meg let part of her mind look as if it, too, had been drugged, while underneath it, she observed. It scared her. Whoever was doing this was powerful. No wonder they were taking over the Islands.

Ruth was right. She found Meg within minutes of her arriving at the Temple. Meg had to admit to herself that she was so happy to see Ruth she almost hugged her. Ruth put a hand on Meg's arm to stop her, nodding at the crowd that was showing only the emotions of delight and happiness.

Meg understood. They would have stood out. They both kept their minds still as they slowly backed out of the crowd. As soon as they were out of sight, they shifted.

Meg stuck with being a raven, but instead of a red fox, Ruth also became raven so that they could travel away from the Temple together. Neither one of them thought that the Kai-Via was so stupid as to not leave spies on the lookout for anyone not following the rules of Aaron-Lem, so birds seemed the safest way to travel.

A few miles away, they landed in a grove of trees and transformed back to two women, a mother and daughter. It was only then that Meg let her feelings show, and Ruth took her in her arms and hugged her.

It had been many years since Meg had cried. Even finding herself stranded in a place that hated her kind, she had kept it together. But seeing the amount of control the Kai-Via had, Meg had finally realized the extent of the danger that she was in. Added to that the fact that she had found herself caring about others, the impact was too much.

For a moment in time, Ruth became the mother she missed, and Meg allowed herself to share her feelings with another.

Twenty-One

Stryker's arrival on the Islands was kept as secret as possible. Instead of arriving at the trading port on Lopel, he arrived in a quiet inlet on Hetale. Two men rowed Stryker to shore, where Ibris waited. Stryker felt mixed emotions looking at the still figure standing on the beach.

He was proud of the man that Ibris had become. He had taught Ibris everything, raising him as if he was his own. Stryker thought that perhaps that was why Ibris was so good at what he did. It was the time he had spent with him after his family died.

Ibris had already been strong and thoughtful, but Stryker had taught him how to overcome his grief and use his innate skills to conquer the minds of everyone around him.

Except Stryker's of course, Ibris was never allowed to go there. Stryker had also taught Ibris how to close his mind to others, too, so that they couldn't do to him what he was doing to them.

Some skills Stryker never taught Ibris. Like the secret to getting into his mind. The last thing Stryker needed was Ibris seeing what he was thinking. Instead, he kept a series of thoughts that Ibris might expect at the forefront of his mind, and never let him past that.

What Ibris didn't know wouldn't hurt him. Or it would—because Stryker was not sure about Ibris. That was his mixed emotion. Had Ibris learned more than he had taught him? Could he read, and influence, anyone's mind? Ibris' tendency to leniency had always been evident, and Stryker knew that it could be a strength instead of a weakness if applied correctly.

But just in case, Stryker had another weapon. Dax. Dax was also his protégé. But Dax could not read and influence minds. Realizing that he didn't have that talent, Stryker fostered the talent Dax did have. The ability to produce terror. Control through fear. The two men were his weapons.

Weapons Stryker hoped he could control long enough to accomplish his mission. After that, he would either let them destroy each other, or step in and do it himself. Or, perhaps he would find a way to save at least one of them. He loved Ibris and Dax, but his mission was more important than his love for them. However, if they remained under his control and fully embraced his mission, he could have both.

As the rowboat came closer, Ibris waded out into the water and helped pull it to shore so that Stryker could step off on the white sand without getting his feet wet. Stryker accepted Ibris' hand as he stepped onto the beach, and was so touched by the gesture he stood with his arm on Ibris' shoulder as they watched the rowboat return to the ship.

Dropping his arm, Stryker slowly turned around, taking in the beauty of Hetale and Lopel which he could see at the end of the narrow band of land the natives called the Arrow.

All the years of staring at a map and daydreaming about this place and he was finally here. The feeling was even more powerful than he had expected. The place was too beautiful to put into words. He could barely take it all in. After weeks of riding in the ship, smelling the men and the salt air, the aroma of flowers drifting down from the white cliffs hit every one of his senses.

Falling to his knees, Stryker bowed his head in gratitude. Ibris stood by awkwardly and then fell to his knees beside him, and together they thanked Aaron, the God of Aaron-Lem, for bringing them both safely to this land of so much beauty.

To Ibris, it was a chance to show Stryker what he could accomplish without killing, and to Stryker, it was the end of one hunt and the beginning of another. The final one, because the Islands held the key to his ultimate power.

Even Aaron would fall under his rule. He would keep Aaron-Lem as a tool to control people, but he, Stryker, would become the God. After all, he and Aaron had created this one true religion together. But in the end, it would only be him left to enforce it. He never let himself think of the third man who had created it with them. That man was no longer counted.

Stryker took a deep breath and spun around with his arms to the sky, praising Aaron for the beauty. He thought it was the right touch, showing Ibris his loyalty to Aaron. After a few more minutes, Ibris asked if Stryker was ready to go to his rooms. Stryker nodded, and Ibris led him across the sands to the stairs carved in the cliffs.

Both of them were aware that Mages had carved out the steps using their magic, but neither acknowledged it. There was no point in destroying what was useful, like the steps, just because before magic was outlawed, magic built it.

From the boat, the cook and his men watched the two tiny figures walk up the cliffs and then disappear into the trees that grew to the edge. Only then did they signal for the rowboat to be lowered again.

Silently two men from the crew rowed Leon and the others across. Leon wasn't worried. No one would give them away.

Stryker was universally hated. Without being told what the cook and his men were up to, the sailors hoped it was something that would return their free way of life to them.

Aaron-Lem was something to be tolerated, but not loved. It had destroyed too many of their families and taken their hope away. They wanted to be free from the fog that the Kai-Via could generate, and the words of the Preacher. They had never been fooled. They had only been afraid.

No words were spoken as the men stepped off the rowboat and onto the shore. Everything that there was to say had been communicated without words. They bowed to each other and then Leon and his eight men turned to the steps as the two crew members returned to their ship.

Hidden in a clump of bushes at the top of the cliff, Tarek and Silke had watched both arrivals. Once the nine men had climbed the steps to the top of the cliff, Tarek stepped out of the bushes, Silke flying behind him.

Leon's face broke into a huge smile, and the two of them rushed at each other and into an embrace. Tarek stepped back and stared into Leon's face, so like his own. "Welcome cousin," he said.

The men gave a silent "whoop," seeing the reunion. It was one more step accomplished in their plan. There were many more to take, but they were determined to succeed, no matter what the odds or the danger.

Twenty-Two

Meg and Ruth arrived at the cave just as Trin began its journey across a clear blue sky. After their day on Hetale, they had agreed to travel together to the next meeting. However, instead of leaving right away, they had to wait until the following day. There was still the problem that all of Meg's abilities vanished with nightfall.

Meg tried to make light of it, but it felt as if another part of her was being ripped away. First, she had lost her home, her parents, her sister, and now her identity. Meg defined herself as a shapeshifter. Take that away, and what was she? Ordinary. She wasn't sure if she wanted to live as an Ordinary. What fun would that be?

And even though Meg knew it had been her choice to leave her family behind, she still felt as if it was unfair that she had to make the choice to leave. A choice which resulted in being banished to a place that took her power away.

It was not something she voiced out loud to her new friends. She had a feeling they would not approve of her fear of being Ordinary. *But then they weren't were they? So what did they know?*

Ruth had stayed the night in the old building with her, which was much more pleasant than Meg thought it would be.

Ruth listened without judgment to what Meg's life used to be like.

It was an odd feeling for Meg not to have to worry about getting in trouble with her words, or for her past. The two of them had tried to figure out what was on the Islands, or all of Thamon, that took Meg's magic away at nightfall.

It didn't happen to anyone else that they knew. There was nothing obvious, and Ruth told Meg that for now she would just have to put up with it.

Perhaps it had something to do with the Kai-Via, and they would discover the solution as they worked to dismantle it and stop Stryker.

It was a few days later before it dawned on Meg that Ruth had listened carefully to her, but she had never told Meg anything about her own previous life. *Of course*, Meg thought, *I didn't ask her anything either, and maybe I should have.*

Meg and Ruth had flown to the cave as ravens and landed in the trees that flanked the entrance. They watched Tarek coming down the steps, Silke hovering beside him blinking on and off. Both of them were surprised when Tarek looked up at them and waved.

"How did you know that it was us?" Ruth asked, once they had flown down to the cave entrance and returned to their true form.

"Well, I took a chance that the two ravens I saw in the tree, were the two of you. On the other hand, it could have been just two random ravens trying to make friends. Either way, it wouldn't have mattered."

Meg gave Tarek a look, which only made him laugh. Meg felt like transforming herself back into a raven and pulling his hair, but instead just huffed and sat down on one of the steps. A few minutes later, Wren and Roar arrived.

"Do you want to fly through the cave, or take the boat?" Tarek asked them.

When no one answered, Wren spoke up. "Boat. Let's keep our shifting to a minimum. We don't know how much our changing might also be shifting the energy around us, and someone could pick up on it."

Tarek smiled at Wren as he extended his hand to help her down into the boat. As he did so, he whispered in her ear, "Wise beyond your years, or older than you look?"

Wren's face registered a moment of shock, but she quickly composed herself. "I could ask the same of you, Tarek."

He nodded in agreement and turned his attention to helping the rest of them into the boat. Meg refused to take his hand, which only made him laugh at her again.

"Be careful you don't start a fire, young lady," Tarek said.

Silke giggled as she slipped into a pocket in his jacket.

"Don't you get tired of that thing blinking on and off?" Meg sniped in return.

Everyone turned to look at Meg, who glared back at them.

Wren moved until she was standing directly in front of Meg. The boat rocked as she stood there, water sloshing over the sides enough to make the seats uncomfortably damp.

"Would you like to get off the boat right now, Meg? You can either treat everyone with respect or make a go of it on your own. It doesn't much matter to me. And I doubt if it matters much to anyone else."

Meg stared back at her, not knowing what to do. This was new territory for her. She heard a soft voice in her head say, "Meg, be wise. Say you are sorry."

Trembling, Meg took a deep breath and whispered, "'I'm sorry."

"Not just to me, Meg. To everyone, and especially Silke."

Meg looked over at Ruth. She knew it was her that had spoken to her. Ruth smiled, and Meg turned to everyone and said, "'I'm sorry."

"And Silke?" Wren pushed.

Silke had made it easier for Meg because she had flown over to Wren and was now sitting on her shoulder.

"I know, my on and off light can be annoying. Would it be easier for you if I turned myself off or down?"

"You can do that?" Meg asked.

In response, Silke turned off, but Meg could see that it meant she could barely move.

"No, stop it. I'm sorry, really. I wish I could turn a light on like that."

Wren looked at Meg to make sure she was serious. When she was satisfied, she turned to Tarek and said, "I think we're ready now."

Tarek winked and started the boat moving through the cave. Meg had reached out an open palm, and Silke had landed on it, and now the two of them sat together, Meg looking strangely comforted by Silke's presence and her on and off blinking.

"We're not stopping?" Roar asked, as the boat practically flew through the cave, barely touching the water.

Tarek shook his head and pointed to where they were heading.

"I have someone I want you to meet."

A few minutes later, the boat glided out of the cave and into a lake that was so still it looked like blue glass. Towering white cliffs flanked it—cliffs with no stairs in them.

Taking in the beauty, Meg realized it was the perfect place to hide. The only way in was by air or cave. And of course, you would have to know about the cave to even start to look for it.

It was so peaceful and beautiful that Meg almost missed the

men standing at the edge of the lake waiting for them. Big men, nine of them.

She held her breath until Tarek waved at them, and the man standing in the front waved back. Friends.

Twenty-Three

Meg picked up a stone by the lake and tried skimming it across the water. She had seen people in Erda do it all the time, but she had never figured it out. *All these magical skills and I can't do this,* she thought.

She was passing the time waiting for the "meeting" to start. Meetings were something she never thought she would find herself attending. Life was to be lived, not meeting with people to figure something out.

For Meg, there had never been something to figure out. She could be anyone she wanted to be at any time. There were no rules for someone like her.

Turns out that was then, and maybe never again, Meg thought, shivering at the thought. Of course, if she could find a portal maker, she could have him send her somewhere else. Perhaps not back to Erda, but somewhere where she could be free again.

"Hey, Meg," Silke called as she flew to Meg's shoulder. In the intense light of Trin, Silke's blinking was barely noticeable, but the rest of her made up for it. How she flew was not visible to the eye. In fact, it was a mystery to Meg. Although Silke's hair looked like feathers, they were not wings. And even though

Silke was shaped somewhat like a small bird, her face reminded Meg of a china doll she had once had, before she had smashed it to bits to see what was inside of it.

"I hope you are not going to smash me to bits to see what's inside of me," Silke said.

Catching the look on Meg's face, she added, "Whoops, sorry, didn't mean to be listening in. Do you want me to leave you alone?"

"No. No, I won't smash you to bits to see what's inside of you, but to make up for sneaking around in my head, you could tell me some things I want to know."

"Like what? I can't tell you secrets. I never tell secrets. And I can't lie. So sometimes I can't answer at all if it would mean I have to lie."

Meg looked at the blinking, fluffy, china doll with feather hair floating in front of her face and realized that she had never met anyone like her. She never told secrets? She couldn't lie?

Silke could be someone she could confide in and not worry about what would happen. And she already knew that Silke was loyal. Look how she had almost died trying to find Tarek.

Tarek, that's what she wanted to know. Who was he?

"I won't tell you Tarek's story, Meg. It's his story to tell, just as yours is yours to tell. But I can tell you that I am bound to him for my life or his life. So even though he thought he was doing me a favor by keeping me away from danger, he put me in danger."

Silke, glanced over at Tarek talking to the men. "But he learned his lesson. He'll never do it again."

"But you can tell me that he's a wizard, right? What kind of wizard? What can he do? And then who are those men?"

"Still questions better answered by them. I can tell you about me. You can tell me about you. And I can tell you about things you don't know, but right now you don't know enough to ask them."

When Meg glared at her, Silke added, "And being angry at me is not going to get you anywhere."

With those words, Silke disappeared, leaving Meg feeling even more upset than she had before. She reached down and grabbed a handful of rocks and tossed them into the lake, not caring that they marred the perfect stillness of the waters. Each stone producing multiple circles that spread out over the lake before disappearing.

"That's what you do, isn't it?" Wren said, coming up to stand beside her.

"What is this? Advice day?" Meg huffed, and after pausing, asked, "What do you mean anyway?"

"You act, and react, and make ripples and circles that affect people and you don't stop to think about what it has done, or will do to anyone, even yourself."

"How do you know? You don't know me!"

"I know you better than you think. I've watched you. You take food and clothes. Do you care what happens to the people you steal from? I know how you got here on Thamon. You ran away. Did you stop and think about how that would affect the people you left behind?

"You don't need to answer me, Meg. I already know the answer. The question is whether or not you can change. Yes, you can shift and be anyone you want to be. But can you change yourself into someone that matters?"

"If you don't like me, why bother with me at all?"

"Did I say I don't like you? Besides, it doesn't matter if I, or any of us like you, does it? At least not to you. But to answer your question, we bother with you, because we hope that somewhere inside that selfish act that you put on, there is someone else that cares."

Softening her tone a little, Wren turned to look at Meg. "I don't think you are here with us just for self-preservation. I think you are here because you want to be more. Perhaps being sent here was more than the portal maker wanting to punish you for your arrogance. Perhaps there is a bigger plan—one where we need you to help us stop Aaron from destroying magic and the freedom to be anyone we want to be.

"Perhaps without you, we won't succeed. However, it will be up to you to decide."

Wren started to walk away and then turned and added, "And for what it's worth, Meg. I do like you. The real you. It's there. I hope you will decide to stop running and become yourself, because I think you and I could be friends."

Meg stared after Wren feeling a roll of emotions. Friends? Did she know what a friend was, or did? Both Silke and Wren, and even Ruth had offered her the gift of friendship, but what did that mean?

It seemed dangerous. But perhaps not as dangerous as being alone.

Twenty-Four

Standing behind one of the Temple pillars so he couldn't be seen, Dax watched Stryker and Ibris walking back and forth. Both of them had their hands clasped behind their backs, sometimes talking, other times walking silently side by side.

It made his head hurt watching them. They looked so much alike. They could have been father and son. It didn't seem fair. He would never be mistaken for Stryker's son.

While both of them were fair and blue-eyed, he was dark and close to the ground. His brown eyes were so dark, people often thought they were black until they saw him angry, then his eyes flashed with flakes of gold.

Stryker had taken both of them under his wing and nurtured them. At first, the two of them had enjoyed each other's company as much as they enjoyed being one of Stryker's chosen few.

But Ibris quickly learned Stryker's techniques of mind control, whereas Dax never understood the need to hide the real message beneath charm and words people wanted to hear.

The more he struggled, the angrier he got, losing all hope of being one of Stryker's preachers. Instead, Dax became a soldier, a warrior. Dax wasn't stupid. He knew he was doing it to earn

Stryker's admiration and praise. At the same time, he couldn't help himself. He needed to cause chaos and pain.

Making war against the enemies of Aaron-Lem fit Dax perfectly. He had a righteous cause to fight for. It was Stryker's cause too. Sooner or later, Stryker would understand that his brand of conversion was far more effective than what Ibris wanted.

What are they talking about? Dax fumed to himself. After watching for what felt like hours, he couldn't take it anymore. Watching the two of them strolling together as if there was not a bigger mission to accomplish made his blood boil.

Dax knew Stryker didn't like to be interrupted, but Dax had waited long enough. He needed to know the plan. Could he kill the people they had locked away yet? He would have done it long ago, but Ibris insisted that was not the way. If it had been up to Ibris, those people who practiced magic would never even have been locked up. They would have been converted or subdued by Ibris' words.

Taking those people and their families as prisoners was a compromise between the two of them. However, Dax knew what was going on with the treatment of the prisoners, and Ibris and Stryker did not. Heavily drugged, often beaten, rarely fed, they were not going to survive anyway.

Taking a deep breath, Dax strode out to meet the two of them. His presence was so intense that he scattered the birds and butterflies, causing both Stryker and Ibris to look at him in astonishment. Ibris' face turned to disapproval, but Stryker immediately returned to his stoic face. If Dax hadn't known Stryker as well as he did, he would have thought that his disruption had not bothered Stryker.

But Dax had seen the flash of fire in Stryker's blue eyes, and for a moment he was afraid. But instead of showing his fear,

Dax showed his control. He smiled at the two of them and asked pleasantly if he could join them. Perhaps they could point out some of the flowers that grew there that he wasn't familiar with?

Stryker took one look at Dax and burst out laughing. "Well, done, son."

All three of them knew what Stryker meant. Dax had commanded the situation. Perhaps he didn't have fancy words to mesmerize people into believing things or doing things they wouldn't otherwise think or do, but he did have other abilities.

"We were just talking about increasing the conversion ceremonies from once a week to twice a week. It looks as if this quiet takeover idea of Ibris' is working. What do you think, Dax?" Stryker asked.

"It has been strangely effective," Dax responded, being careful not to show his frustration. "However, perhaps it is a bit too slow? There are faster ways to convert people, as we have shown throughout Thamon."

"Yes," Ibris responded. "But at what cost? Besides the death toll, thousands of acres of precious forests are dead. Farmland has been polluted. And the grief of the people for those they lost will never heal. We will always have the potential of a rebellion on our hands.

"Doing it my way, the Islands remain fertile and beautiful, and the people are happy. We still control them, but not through fear but through making them believe that this is all for them."

"And you don't think that someday they will wake up and rebel anyway?" Dax responded. "What if your pretty words and hidden suggestions stop working? We could all be killed while we look away, thinking that your soft ways will succeed."

The two men were squared off to each other, Stryker

watching them both. Listening. He loved this conflict. These two men were his favorites of all the men he had trained.

He never bothered to try and teach the women. They were to be used and tossed aside and never given power. They were much too devious and hard to read. No, only men suited his purposes, and these two were the best.

The fact that they stood at different sides of the issue pleased Stryker. It was precisely what he had hoped would happen. He didn't care who won. Either way, he did. Thamon would be his, and whoever remained standing would be there with him. Side by side. Ruling this amazing world.

That is if they survived the process. That was always debatable. Stryker clapped them both on the back and said, "Love these discussions, but let's table it for now, and get something to eat. Make nice and let's go."

Neither of the two men moved. Finally, Ibris placed his hand on Dax's shoulder and said, "Let's go eat, cousin. We have plenty of time."

That's just it, Dax thought to himself. *We don't. Once Stryker gets what he wants we will both be expendable, and none of your pretty words can change that.*

The word "cousin" felt wrong to Ibris, but it was true. Their fathers were brothers. And Stryker had always wanted to take both their fathers' places in their hearts. He could let Stryker think he had succeeded, but it wasn't true, No one could.

Then there was the fact that Ibris knew that Stryker was on the Islands for a reason other than converting these two tiny islands to Aaron-Lem.

No, there was something else happening. What it was, Ibris didn't know. But no matter what it was, he had two people to watch out for—his cousin and his mentor.

Ibris was reasonably sure that neither one of them were on

his side. He would have to be very careful now. One slip and it would all crash down on his head.

Yes, it was slower to convert the people his way, but it was so much safer. For everyone.

Twenty-Five

Another hour went by before anyone came to ask Meg to join the rest of them. They had all gone to join the nine men talking to Tarek, but Meg hung back.

Did they think she would come on her own? Join them just to be rebuffed?

But eventually Ruth found Meg sitting near the cave entrance hidden by one of the large rock formations that flanked the cave. Like the night before, Ruth didn't say anything, just sat with Meg, waiting.

"I don't know how to be friends, Ruth," Meg eventually said.

"Most people don't. We all have to learn."

"But you seem to do it without any effort."

"I'm old. But not just old, seasoned. I have lived through more heartbreaks than I can count but even more, I have lived with joy and happiness. And over the years, I discovered that both heartbreaks and happiness are easier with a friend or two by my side."

"That's what I mean," Meg said. "I don't know how to be a friend. I never had one. I didn't need one."

"I think that you are probably wrong. Maybe you have never been a friend to someone else, but I know that people have been friends to you. You didn't arrive here on Thamon looking uncared for."

Meg leaned back against the cold stone wall and thought about what Ruth had said. Ruth was right. No matter what she did, her parents had always come through, even when she insisted on calling herself Megladon because it sounded scary and important.

But she had thought they did that because she was their daughter. *Isn't that what parents did? Was that how a friend behaved too?*

And then there was her sister, Suzanne. Meg had harbored both jealousy and disdain for Suzanne, and Suzanne had responded by being there whenever Meg got herself in trouble. Even when she wasn't in trouble, Suzanne was always willing to help her.

It was hard to think of Suzanne without feeling jealous again. Meg had always thought that Suzanne was their parents' favorite daughter. Suzanne behaved herself. Did the right thing. Didn't mind rules.

But the disdain Meg had felt for Suzanne seemed oddly silent. Maybe the lack of magical powers that descended on her every night was shifting her point of view.

Before, she had thought of Suzanne as less than her because Suzanne could only shapeshift to one thing, a dragon. Although even in her jealousy, Meg thought Suzanne's dragon was magnificent.

However, being just one thing had seemed to Meg to be a weakness. If you couldn't be anything or anyone, what good was it to be a shapeshifter?

"So you had friends, even though they were family?" Ruth asked. Meg had left her thoughts open for Ruth, so she wouldn't have to voice them out loud.

"I guess," Meg answered. "I thought they had to act that way because we are family."

"But you didn't act that way, did you?" Ruth responded, not unkindly.

"No, I didn't."

"So what did they do that you didn't do?"

"They cared about me, even though sometimes I was a problem? Well, always a problem, but they were still there for me. Is that a friend? Because if it is, I have never been a friend to anyone."

"And now, you would like to be?"

"To be honest, I'm not sure. But I think so. Still, I think it may be because I know I can't survive here by myself."

Meg looked over at the group huddled around a fire, laughing. She smelled something cooking. Something inside her wished that she was part of that group, not separate from them because her abilities made her feel superior. What abilities did she have anyway? The ability to get in trouble, be flashy, show off, trick people, steal, and get away with it?

"Well, you might be able to turn those attributes into something useful, and not just for you," Ruth said. "Perhaps, for that group of people waiting for us to join them. Learn something about each of them. Get to know them. See if you would be willing to do for them as you do for yourself.

"I think you are ready, Meg. It's just a new skill to develop and one that is much more useful in the long run than something you were born with, but never learned how to use for good."

Meg looked over at Ruth, who when she was not a fox or a raven was what Meg might have previously said looked like anyone. She would have lumped her into the mass of people that meant nothing to her.

But this time she saw Ruth's kind gray eyes and felt something else. It both scared her and thrilled her.

"Want to be my friend, Meg?" When Meg nodded, she added, "Okay, friend, help me up. This stone is cold."

Meg laughed, stood, and extended a hand. When Ruth stood, she reached over and hugged Meg. This time, instead of dissolving into tears as she had the night before, Meg returned the hug.

On the other side of the lake, Tarek was watching. *That Ruth is a marvel,* he thought. *And Meg might be the missing piece that we need to pull this off.*

Leon saw Tarek watching the exchange and asked, "So who is that girl?"

"Someone who doesn't belong here and yet here she is. Now all she has to do is choose to be here, and with us. Not an easy task for her, but it looks as if the first steps are happening, thanks to Silke, Wren, and Ruth."

"Can we do it, Tarek?" Leon asked.

Tarek didn't answer, just watched Ruth and Meg walk around the lake talking together. Meg was actively engaged in listening to Ruth. That in itself was a small miracle. There was no reason there couldn't be more of them.

Twenty-Six

Stryker was taking his time, even though part of him wanted to start the search the minute he stepped onto Hetale. But he had waited all these years, and a few more days were just a drop in the bucket when he found what he was looking for.

He needed everyone to believe that he had come to the Islands to see how the conversion process was going. In spite of himself, he was amazed by how well Ibris was doing with his non-violent conversion.

The news that they needed more ceremonies to accommodate all the people claiming Aaron as their one true God, and Aaron-Lem as the only way to live, was a victory. Besides, it would make his search much more manageable. Fewer people to worry about disrupting it.

For now, he needed to pay attention to what Ibris and Dax were doing. He knew neither could be fully trusted. For different reasons.

If they ever got together in their disagreements, they would be a powerful team. But he had trained them carefully in ways that would make sure they would always be at odds, keeping their focus on where he wanted it to be—on each other, and not on him.

The fact that they were cousins made it even more fun for Stryker to divide them. The two men looked completely different, but that was because Dax took after his mother and not his father.

Training them had been a pleasure for Stryker. They were both focused and driven, just as he had thought they would be. Besides, once they became orphans, they needed him.

If Ibris and Dax ever found out the part he played in the tragedy of losing their families, they might combine their strengths against him. But they never would. He had made sure of that.

Still, even though the conversions were going well, Stryker remained cautious. Although there had been no hint of rebellion on either Island, Stryker was much too wise in the ways of human nature to not think that there would be people plotting to take back the thoughts of the people.

Somebody would see beyond the contentment that people felt under the spell of the Preacher and the doctrines of Aaron-Lem. Not everyone was taken in by the techniques they used to mesmerize the populace.

Besides the hypnotic nature of his teachings, Stryker had taught Dax and Ibris the tools of separation and distraction. Ibris liked the distraction of something good for the people. Dax enjoyed the distraction of cruelty. Both worked.

Of course, it was Dax, following the tenants of Aaron-Lem, who had demanded that all people with any magical ability be immediately removed from the population of Hetale, and Ibris had to comply. Now they needed to do the same in Lopel.

The fact that there were fewer Mages to remove on Lopel was interesting. Either they were already captured, or they were in hiding. The last was the most likely scenario, which is why Stryker's next order of business, besides the search for his treasure, was to begin to track them down.

But first, he needed to see where Dax had hidden the prisoners. Knowing Dax, they were not being cared for, a fact he was hiding from Ibris. Not that Stryker cared about the prisoners' condition.

What he cared about was if anyone would find them, because if they did, they would try and rescue them. Stryker did not want that outcome. It was imperative not to allow anyone to find out about what had happened to the disappearing people.

Yes, it had been noticed that people were disappearing. From what Ibris had told him, there were too many deserted homes on Hetale to go unnoticed. However, Ibris had managed to turn thoughts away from the missing by bringing more people into the embrace of Aaron-Lem.

And Dax had wisely taken all the members of a Mage's family to the prison, leaving no one behind to look for relatives. Friends would look, but would soon come to believe that the missing were gone of their own choice, and were happy somewhere else.

What bothered Stryker the most was that he had no idea where Dax had put the prisoners. Where on the islands could Dax have built a facility to house all those people? Was Dax keeping secrets from him?

On the other hand, the idea that perhaps visiting the prisoners might also lead him towards what he was looking for, excited him. Maybe he would kill two birds with one stone.

Although Stryker knew that Dax was probably letting the prisoners die a slow death, Stryker thought it would be better to kill them and dispose of their bodies so that no one would ever find them. The lie that they were living somewhere else would then become true. Yes, they would be living wherever death took them.

Stryker snorted. Not that he believed that there was anything after death. That was just a bunch of made-up nonsense used to control the people. If there were something after death, then he would deal with it when he got there. But for now, there was just the present, and he was going to get everything he could out of it.

Even Aaron didn't believe the doctrines of Aaron-Lem. What he and Aaron had done was to design a perfect religion that would satisfy everyone. Well, almost everyone. There were those Mages after all.

But for the rest of the people, all they had to do was follow its rules, and they would always have everything they needed. Break the rules, and they would be condemning themselves. It was brilliant.

Stryker bowed to the East where Aaron claimed to be living, which made it the place where all power resided. Anyone watching would have thought that Stryker was following the practice of Aaron-Lem of honoring Aaron three times a day by bowing in his direction. Instead, Stryker had his face to the ground, trying to control the laughter that threatened to take over.

He was so close. Only a few more things to do and they would be bowing to him, even if they didn't know it. That was fine with him. All he wanted was power. He didn't need to be worshiped.

Being that visible was dangerous, He preferred being discreet and unknown, except to those he had to control. Like Dax and Ibris.

Stryker rose, and straightened his cloak, catching a glimpse of himself in the reflection of the mirror hung in his room. He smiled, and his blue eyes sparked with delight. He looked good.

Now, it was time to get Dax and get this next part over with.

Twenty-Seven

"How are you 'cousins?" Meg asked.

Leon had cooked a fantastic meal for them, and now they were all sitting around the fire together. How Leon cooked such a wonderful meal with such limited resources was a mystery to her. She assumed he had used some magic skills, but she didn't see him do it.

Meg asked the question about being cousins because she thought that was what friends might do. Ask a question and then listen. Although she had been curious about things before, Meg had never decided that finding out the answer was worth bothering with someone. Trying to do things differently, she asked the question not only to be friendly but because she realized she actually was curious.

What made Leon and Tarek cousins? How did they end up on these Islands together? Had they planned it? They must have. But when and how?

Tarek must have read her mind because he smiled at her and said, "That was a good first question, Meg. And so are the rest of them. But I'll let Leon tell you how we are cousins."

Leon and the other eight men from the ship sat together as a group across from the rest of them. They were all big men. Meg hadn't learned any names yet other than Leon's, and she had to admit she was a little afraid of them. They all had the weather-beaten faces of sailors, but other than that and their size, they were all quite different. It was hard to imagine how the nine of them had flown under the radar of Stryker.

One of the eight men started to laugh at that, and then all nine of them shriveled up. Well, they were not actually shriveled up, because nothing really changed. They were the same size, had the same faces, but they appeared so much smaller and ordinary.

"Does that answer that question?" the one who had laughed asked. "And Leon taught us to say a prayer all the time, which if Stryker had been looking inside of us, would have thought we were zealots of Aaron-Lem."

"That's a good prayer for you all to know," Leon said. "Blessed be Aaron, the one true god. Blessed be his holy name."

"But that's wrong," Ruth said. "You can't be praying to that false god, no matter what he says."

Leon smiled at Ruth when he answered, "Trust me, we are not. We are protecting our thoughts. If anyone looks inside our minds, that's what they will see. And they will see us bowing to Aaron three times a day. But that's not what's going on.

"Every day on the ship, we fooled Stryker. I cooked his food, and one of my men tasted it." He pointed to the man who had laughed.

"That's Ted. He knew I hadn't poisoned the food. Stryker thought we were on the ship to serve him. He never suspected that we were not there to follow him. He never saw us look like this."

With those words, all nine men transformed back to the men Meg had seen.

"So you are shapeshifters?" Meg asked.

"No. We are what *you* call Ordinary. We don't have any magical skills the way you think of them. What we do have are ways to make you think you see something that isn't there. Anyone can do it. It just takes practice."

"So you aren't a wizard like Tarek?"

"No. To answer your first question, we are cousins by our mothers, who were both talented in different ways. But it was Tarek's father who is a wizard."

It took a moment to register what Leon had said. "Is? Your father *is* still a wizard? Where is he? And where are your mothers? And do you have brothers and sisters?" Meg asked Tarek.

"I bet you've never asked that many questions at one time in your life before," Tarek laughed.

Meg shook her head, face flushing. She wasn't sure what had happened. All at once, she was interested. Not just trying to do what a friend did, but she wanted to know. It was a strange sensation. Meg wasn't sure if she liked it or not.

Leon looked at Tarek and continued. "I said is, because we aren't sure if his father is still alive. He may have escaped. Our families knew it was coming. They were part of the resistance. But we both came home to find entire towns and all the people left in them destroyed because they refused to follow Aaron.

"All of us survived because we were sailing."

Leon looked at his eight men and then back to Tarek. "We will answer all the rest of your questions in time. But right now we need to prepare a camp, so we have a place to stay.

"This is where having a wizard is going to come in handy. We can build the cabin, once the trees are down, but it would be so much faster if you could get the trees for us, Tarek."

"My pleasure," Tarek said, "But I haven't done this for a while, so I suggest that you all move somewhere else. Where do you want me to ask the trees to gather?"

"We were thinking on that rise to the south," Leon said, pointing to a clearing that Meg hadn't noticed.

"If you could all go back to the other side of the lake, I would be more comfortable," Tarek said. "Including you, Silke."

Once they were all gathered on the north side near the cave opening, the group watched in awe as trees began to move out of the forest that stood between the lake and the cliffs and to stack themselves in the clearing. They looked like arrows moving close to the ground, weaving between the standing trees and making hardly a sound.

Leon leaned over and whispered to Meg, "He is calling only the trees that have died. Before they started moving, they dropped their branches. Later, if you walk back into the woods, you'll see their dead branches lying there."

After what Meg thought was probably an hour, Tarek dropped to his knees, and Silke was beside him within seconds. Leon was not far behind offering him water and holding him up as he brought him closer to the fire and helped him lie down.

"He'll be fine," Leon said. "Just give an hour or two to recover. In the meantime, we need to build us a cabin, in an ordinary way."

He winked at Meg as he said ordinary. She couldn't decide if she should be angry, annoyed, or intrigued. She decided on intrigued.

Twenty-Eight

"I thought we were being careful not to use magic. Aren't you worried that pulling trees out of the forest rang a bell somewhere?" Meg asked Tarek once he recovered.

The cabin was going up quickly. Leon and his men seemed to know what to do without being told. For Meg, it was eye-opening. They weren't using magic, but it looked magical. *Did Ordinaries do that all the time and she had missed it?*

Tarek paused for a moment before answering. "Yes. You're right. We might be, 'ringing a bell' somewhere as you put it, using magic. Especially what I did with the trees. But we needed to get this cabin built today, so Leon and I weighed the alternatives and decided this was best."

"What were the alternatives?"

This time Tarek laughed, and then laughed again at the look on Meg's face.

"I was not laughing at you. Well, perhaps I was. It was interesting to watch you try to decide whether to be mad at me for laughing, or just curious. This 'getting to know people' thing will get more comfortable, Meg, if you let it.

"But I laughed the first time because that was a logical question, and I realized I had started to misjudge you."

"What did you think? That I have no brains in my head because I'm a shapeshifter? Look who is judging who!"

Tarek stuck out his hand and said, "Truce?"

Reluctantly Meg shook his hand. "Still, what alternatives?"

"A dry, cozy cabin, or caught outside in the storm that is coming?"

Meg looked up and saw only a clear blue sky. Obviously Tarek was mistaken, but still, a cozy cabin sounded good. A second later, Silke appeared on Tarek's shoulder and shooed Meg away, saying, "He needs more rest. Besides, Ruth wants you to help gather the food and water we are going to need."

Okay, two delusional people, Meg thought, but she knew she should help. However, instead of walking back to the group, she shifted into a raven and flew over. It was such a joy to fly. She could see how her sister might be content to be only a dragon. A deep sadness came over Meg, surprising her, and shifting her back to her true form so that she fell the last few feet.

Embarrassed, she looked around, but no one seemed to have noticed. As Meg took in the gathering of people, she had the oddest sensation, wondering what it would be like to be in a group like this, permanently, just living together, hiding out together. It surprised her that she even had a moment of thinking that it would be pleasant. She was a wild thing. Once this thing that they called a 'revolution' was over, she would happily return to doing whatever she wanted to do.

Ruth smiled at Meg as she approached the group and asked her whether she wanted to collect water, food, or moss for sealing in between the logs. Meg squashed the immediate response that she was not a slave so she wouldn't be doing any of those things.

Looking around the group, she decided it might be a good time to get to know someone else better. Roar looked like a likely candidate. She hadn't spent any quality time with him yet.

"I'll help Roar with whatever he is doing, as long as he doesn't turn into that mangy yellow cat," Meg said. And then hearing what that sounded like added, "Just kidding, Roar. Sorta."

Ruth gave Meg a look that Meg took to mean that she could have done that better, and then said," Okay. Roar is collecting moss. We need a lot of it. And don't go using magic to get it. We've sent enough magic signals out today. And that includes shifting into other things. Like ravens."

Once again, Meg was caught between embarrassment and anger, but it was Roar who saved her by saying. "That's good. That cat is rather mangy. Let's go to into the woods on the north side of the lake, Meg. That's where we will probably find the most moss."

Roar was right. The combination of more shade from the north and the mist from the cave which opened on the north side of the lake was the perfect combination for large swaths of moss. Meg had the strangest sensation that the moss was waiting for them when they arrived because it was so easy to roll up into bundles. It was as if it had detached itself from the earth in preparation.

She and Roar worked quietly together, rolling up bundles of moss. Once the men saw the rolls of moss on the ground, they took turns coming to get them, leaving Roar and Meg to the easy job of gathering. When Meg realized that Roar was not going to talk unless she asked him a question, she thought about what she most wanted to know, and realized it was how he got his name, Roar.

"It's because I don't have the manner of a lion that you ask, isn't it, Meg?" Roar answered once she got the courage to ask him. "But that's because Roar is not a sound. It's a combination of names. My father was Ron, and my mom was Aria. When they passed away, I put their names together in their honor. I represent them both now. Hence, Roar."

Meg stopped with an armful of moss and looked at Roar. That made much more sense. In his true form, he was a small man, slight, but solid. Old enough to be her father, perhaps. Ages didn't make much sense to her since she was practically ageless in her homeland of Erda.

"Can you shift to anything?" Meg asked, thinking of the different beings he had shifted to, like a yellow cat, a bird, and a much older man. "And what happened to your parents?" She remembered to ask because that was probably more important to him than shifting.

"They passed away a long time ago. I've been Roar all of my adult life. And, no, I can't shift to just anything the way you can, but I can be a few different things. It's enough to be helpful, but not a burden."

When it was apparent that was all that Roar was going to say, Meg went back to gathering moss. She would ask Ruth what happened to Roar's parents. But what gave her pause was him saying the ability to shift to many things could be a burden. That was something that had never occurred to her before.

Was Suzanne freer than she was? Once again, Meg was surprised by the rush of emotions she felt as she realized how much she missed her sister and her parents. Wasn't constantly feeling things a bigger burden than the ability to shift to anyone she wanted to be?

A shout from the cabin woke her from her thoughts. Leon and his men were pointing at the sky. Just a few minutes before it had been a bright blue, now it was gray and getting darker.

A boom of thunder louder than any thunder she had ever heard before echoed throughout the small valley. It was so loud it caused vibrations in the lake.

"Run," she heard in her head. Roar must have heard it too because he gathered the last few rolls of moss and started running. They reached the cabin as the first sheet of water began to sweep across the lake, followed by a flash of lighting so bright that for a brief moment Meg could see the tops of the cliffs.

Then someone grabbed her and Roar, pulled them in, and slammed the door shut, sliding a massive piece of wood across it to keep it closed.

"That's crazy," Meg said. "Are all storms like that here?"

Ruth, Roar, and Wren looked at each other. It was Wren who answered, "No, they're getting worse, and more often. Ever since the Kai-Via arrived. There may be no connection, but we think there is."

Roar mumbled under his breath, "It's almost as if the Islands are trying to clean themselves."

It was Tarek that heard him and added, "Perhaps they are."

Twenty-Nine

Ibris watched the storm from the safety of his room in the Temple. Outside, his garden was taking a beating. Almost everything had been flattened by the wall of water that first swept over the Islands, and then returned to drop more sheets of rain.

It didn't seem possible that so much water could fall from the sky. There had always been storms, but during the warm months, they had always been gentle and welcome. However, recently they had started to become more and more violent, often appearing out of nowhere, and catching too many people by surprise.

As always, Ibris had an internal warning of the approaching storm and had sent the Kai-Via to warn the people. They started with the people with tents and booths on the Arrow. Ibris knew that the people would listen to the Kai-Via, and then associate the warning with the Kai-Via caring about them. It wasn't true for the Kai-Via, but it was true for him.

He did care for the people, and he was grateful that the entire Arrow was cleared before the first wave swept over it.

Ibris knew that Dax would use the storm to notice who knew ahead of time that it was coming. Dax kept a small notebook with him at all times where he kept the names of people who seemed more than Ordinary. Ibris hoped that the people had enough sense to hide their awareness until the Kai-Via warned them. He thought that perhaps they did because he was sure there were still Mages on the Islands. But none had been captured recently.

Earlier that day, Ibris had felt a swell of magic on Lopel. It had lasted about an hour and then stopped. Hopefully, no one else had noticed, but he wasn't so naive as to think he was the only one who knew when magic was being practiced.

Ibris held a small glass globe in his hand. It was this globe that told him of the coming storm. Or at least that was what he told everyone else. When a storm like the one they were having approached, the globe would turn dark, and a miniature storm would rage within it. The other times, it was clear and empty. The globe was allowed by Aaron and Stryker because it saved lives. Anyone could use it, even though it belonged to Ibris and his family. Somehow that made it not magic.

What no one had noticed was it only worked when Ibris was nearby. Luckily, on the Islands, he was always close enough to produce a storm inside of the ball when he knew a storm was coming.

There was no magic in the ball, but he loved it anyway. It had been his mother's. She loved producing scenes inside of it and making up stories to share with the village children.

When Ibris' village was destroyed by what Stryker had said was an earthquake and then burned to the ground, Ibris had seen the glint peeking out from the mud. He doubled over in pain, clasping the glass ball in his hand as he curled up in the mud with only the desire of death in his mind.

It was Stryker who found him there, rescued him, and brought him back to his home. Later Stryker had rescued Dax from his village which had also been destroyed by that same earthquake.

At first, Ibris had accepted everything that Stryker told them. As he grew older, he wondered how both their villages had looked the same after being destroyed. Was it really an earthquake? He might never know for sure, but he suspected that Stryker had somehow made it happen because he had wanted the two of them, for his own reasons.

Over the years, Stryker had brought home many other young boys, rescued from the disasters of their villages. But Dax and Ibris had risen to the top of his chosen ones. Or so they had been told.

Ibris wasn't all that sure it was true. He knew that Stryker and Aaron had been planning the takeover of Aaron-Lem for a long time. He knew that there were other Kai-Via in other parts of Thamon doing his bidding. Other Preachers. Other men like Dax programmed to love war and killing.

Thunder shook the walls of his home. Lightning lit the sky, and Ibris could see that the Arrow was now completely underwater. That meant the two Islands were, for the time being, separate. Ibris was grateful for the storm. His garden would recover, the people were safe, and it delayed Stryker's search for the treasure that Ibris believed Stryker had come to find.

Yes, Ibris knew about the map. He had found it years ago when he was still young and naive enough to believe in Stryker as a good, kind man.

Stryker had taken the map out of his pocket where he always kept it. He'd been called out of the room, not knowing that Ibris was standing outside the door. It was only curiosity that had impelled Ibris to look at the map.

He hadn't known what it was then, but later he would

figure it out. Now, he believed that he knew why Stryker was in Hetale. And it wasn't just to convert the people. He had a more personal, and much more dangerous, reason than that.

Ibris saw himself as the Stonenut tree. Strong, yielding when necessary, but always straight and true. Somehow he would defeat Stryker and his bands of Kai-Via, and Aaron with his evil intent of being the only real God. Ibres knew there was one God, but it was most certainly not Aaron. And it was that one God that Ibris served.

In the meantime, he bided his time. He was doing his best to save the people in the only way he knew how at the moment.

But Ibris was worried that between Stryker and Dax, his time might be running out.

Thirty

Dax was not happy about showing Stryker where he was holding his prisoners. For the past few months, he had been gathering anyone who could do any form of magic. Dax took them, and all of their family, to the prison camp he had built on Hetale.

To Dax, it didn't matter if all they could do was coax a glass off the shelf, he considered them magical. It hadn't been hard to find those people. All he had to do was sit in the Market and listen. Sometimes he would talk to the people walking by, or shopping at the Market.

They hadn't known that he was part of the Kai-Via and even if they had known, at that time it probably wouldn't have changed anything. They were a friendly people, happy to share who they were, even with strangers.

A month later, when the Kai-Via officially arrived, they would never have thought the stranger they had been friendly with was the head of the Kai-Via that would imprison them.

The deception had been an easy one. Members of the Kai-Via arrived on the trading ships. Although there were eight of them, including the Preacher, they didn't all come on the same boat. They had staggered their arrivals.

Ibris and Dax were both the first to arrive and had then done the same thing, mixed with the people.

For Ibris, it had been about getting to know the people and how they behaved so that he could tune his sermons to how they heard things, and what they needed. Dax wanted to know the same things, but not for the same reasons.

Ibris wanted to convert them without bloodshed, and Dax wanted to find out how to cause war. Even though the conversion was Ibris' way right now, it wouldn't always be his way. Dax was going to make sure of that.

Taking away the magical people had been child's play for Dax and his team. He already knew who they were, having met them at the Market. The people were not expecting to be taken prisoner and had nothing to fear when a group of young men arrived at their door and asked if they could tell them about Aaron-Lem. Almost everyone invited the handsome young men into their homes and even offered them food. Later, when they woke up in their cold prison cells, none of them had a memory of how they got there.

If Dax had a heart, perhaps he would have felt some pang of sorrow for his prisoners as they wept and moaned in their drug-induced state. For them, it was a nightmare that they couldn't wake up from. For Dax, it was a bother that they were still alive.

Dax would have preferred a more aggressive approach to taking prisoners, but then Ibris would have become more concerned and called a halt to what he was doing. As it was, Ibris thought that all the people had been escorted to a camp on the far side of Hetale, and were living there peacefully, although even Ibris knew they had to be drugged so they wouldn't escape by using their magical abilities.

The shapeshifters were the worst. They had to be heavily drugged because otherwise they could shift into something else and escape—especially those shapeshifters who could be anything. Dax was taking no chances with them, and because they were so heavily drugged and chained, many of them were on the verge of death. Some had already died. *Less to worry about,* Dax thought.

But right now, Dax *was* worried. He wasn't sure what Stryker would say about the prison camp. They had never discussed the treatment of prisoners before. There was a chance that Stryker would be furious. *On the other hand, he could be impressed,* Dax thought. Maybe with Stryker's permission, he could torture and then kill some of them on purpose. Dax was trying to look on the bright side of having to show Stryker the camp.

The Preacher and none of the other Kai-Via knew where the camp was located. The only people who did were the few men that Dax trusted. He had recruited them throughout the years as he served with them in the armies of Aaron-Lem. They were the ones that had gone out into cities, towns, villages, and the countryside and "converted" people by force. The conversion consisted of the choice of either become a worshiper of the one true God, Aaron, or die.

Not that Dax cared about the one true God part. All he knew was that people had to believe in something, why not Aaron? After all, Stryker had chosen to follow Aaron, and since Dax owed Stryker his life, he would do what he wanted him to do. Most of the time.

But it was the fighting that Dax loved. He would have been just as happy fighting for any other man that claimed to be a god. It gave him pleasure that he could serve someone like Stryker while he did it. However, in the end, Dax just needed a reason to fight.

In the beginning, Ibris had been part of that kind of conversion process but soon made it clear that he hated every minute of it. He was a weak coward as far as Dax was concerned. It was hard to believe that at one point he and Ibris had thought of each other as more than cousins. They were brothers. No longer. Ibris had grown soft while Dax had gotten stronger.

Dax had planned to take Stryker to the prisoner camp in the most indirect way possible. His hope was that Stryker would never be able to find the site again, or along the way change his mind and decide not to go. When Stryker pulled a map of the Island out of his pocket, Dax knew that plan wouldn't work. He could only hope that Stryker was on his side once he saw how he treated the prisoners. If not, he wasn't sure what he was going to do.

They were on their way to the camp when the storm hit. Neither of them saw it coming. The dark sky, thunder, and sheet of water arrived at almost the same time. Luckily they were near a cave that Stryker had marked on the map as something he wanted to see, and they pushed the horses as hard as they could to get there.

It took only a few minutes, but by the time they arrived, they were drenched. The opening of the cave was high enough to bring the horses inside. They hitched the horses and then stepped back further in the cave to wait out the storm.

Later, after the storm passed, Dax watched Stryker make a note on the map, and look happier than he had ever seen him. Dax hoped that Stryker's happiness would last once they got to the prison camp.

Thirty-One

No one needed to tell Stryker that they were near the prison camp. If nothing else, the smell that sometimes drifted their way was enough to give it away. But it was more than that. It felt as if they had entered a dead zone. No birds sang, the trees looked half-dead, and there were no bright flowers that the Islands were famous for anywhere to be seen.

For the first time, Stryker felt a frisson of fear. What had he created with Dax? Had he gone too far? Yes, he had wanted a fearless warrior, and a man who would love to fight, but was there any humanity left in Dax, or only the desire for bloodshed?

Stryker glanced over at Dax and wondered what he would think if he knew the whole truth. *Would Dax then become his enemy?* And if he did, would Dax win? Based on what Dax appeared to have done with the prisoners, he didn't seem to have any remorse left in him at all. Right now Dax served him, but how long would that be true?

The question in Stryker's mind was what to do when they reached the prison camp. It was a delicate choice. He had to keep Dax working for him, and at the same time not give Dax the wrong idea about what he was trying to accomplish.

For a moment, Stryker entertained the thought of killing Dax now before he got too far out of control. It was just the two of them, no one would know. As if he heard his thoughts, Dax glanced over at Stryker and gave him what passed for a smile.

Stryker wasn't worried that Dax had listened to his thoughts. Dax had never gotten the hang of listening in to what people were thinking. Instead, he was a warrior who loved to fight and a brilliant tactician.

That's why Stryker had picked him.

Before launching Aaron-Lem's takeover, Stryker had sent his spies throughout Thamon. He asked them to choose the boys they thought would grow up to serve him best. Stryker had different criteria for what he was looking for, and one of them was what Dax's people were. Fiercely loyal, and never afraid to fight, which had made it particularly hard to destroy the village where Dax lived. Many of his men had died while securing Dax for him.

Aaron had agreed to delay the large scale conversion until Stryker had trained the boys like Ibris and Dax, and had found the men who would be loyal enough to be one of the Kai-Via. Stryker snickered to himself, thinking how stupid people were to think there was only one Kai-Via. How could he control a world with just seven men plus a Preacher? No, he had many groups of Seven headed by a warrior like Dax, who protected the Preachers. But Ibris and Dax were the best, which is why he had sent them to the Islands.

He didn't want a bloody conversion. He wanted the transformation that Ibris was producing. But, he didn't tell Ibris that. Stryker knew that keeping Ibris on edge, not knowing if he would change his mind, was the best way to control what was happening. A peaceful conversion made his search for the treasure much more manageable. He didn't need a war and all the accompanying destruction that would take place.

Which brought Stryker back to Dax. Did he still control Dax? And if not, what should he do about it? Should he let Dax kill all the Mages, and shapeshifters he had captured? And if he did, what would Dax do next? Given that kind of power to kill whenever and whoever he wanted to, it could become addictive.

Perhaps he would let Dax decide, but first, he would apply some of his mind control techniques and see if he could make Dax choose what he wanted him to do. He would have to be subtle. Dax had long ago become aware of Stryker entering his mind to suggest things and had learned how to not pay attention to him. It was the only mind control Dax ever seemed to learn. But it was the one that made him dangerous to Stryker.

This would be a good test. If he could get Dax to do what he wanted him to do, and make him believe that it was his own idea, then there was no need to get rid of him. He didn't want to kill him. He had sunk a lot of time and effort into making Dax into the man he was today. It would be a pity to let that all go to waste.

****

Dax wasn't fooled. But he was worried. He had to figure out what Stryker wanted him to do, and then pretend that he had been influenced by Stryker using his manipulation techniques. In his teens, Dax had learned how to tune both Stryker and Ibris, and any of the other mind manipulators, out of his thoughts.

That was the easy part. The hard part was pretending that their techniques were working on him. That meant he had to read the signals and give them what they wanted, fooling them into thinking that they still had a mental power over him.

Would Stryker want him to kill the prisoners? From the micro looks on Stryker's face, Dax could tell that Stryker was not happy about the smell as they neared the camp. Did that mean he didn't understand why Dax had kept them alive, or was he upset over the treatment of the prisoners?

It was going to be easy to pass off the blame to the men guarding the camp. He could claim ignorance of what they had done, and promise that it would never happen again. But what should he say to Stryker? What was Stryker trying to manipulate him into doing?

If he made a mistake, he knew what Stryker would try to do. He wouldn't succeed, of course, but it would ruin his plans. Dax needed Stryker to believe in him for a little while longer.

Besides, now he was curious what was going on with that map that Stryker was so carefully guarding.

Keeping his hand on the knife in his pocket, Dax told Stryker what he thought Stryker wanted to hear. As Stryker turned to him, Dax hoped he had said the right thing.

Thirty-Two

In the end, Dax chose to be bad to look good. Being bad wasn't hard, but he did have some regret that he had to sacrifice some of his men to appear to be good for Stryker.

The prison camp had looked even worse than he had imagined, or even agreed to, which made his decision easier. Once they crested the hill that overlooked the camp, they could see the destruction. Everything was gray. Bodies lay on the ground outside the prison cells in various stages of decay.

Stryker's gasp when he saw it was enough to confirm to Dax what he needed to do. Plead ignorance. In some ways, he was. He had no idea that it had gotten so bad. It seemed that once the men had been given carte blanche to mistreat or ignore the prisoners as much as they wanted to, they went from being soldiers to savages.

Which made it easy for Dax to blame the conditions of the camp on his men, and then have them killed. Dax thought that it was probably for the best. They had lost all sense of duty, and he wasn't so sure he could bring them back to the fighting conditions that he needed them for anyway.

First, Dax had the soldiers clean up the camp, bury the dead, wash out all of the prison rooms, clean the prisoners, and give them food and water. In some ways, that was more of a punishment for the soldiers than what came next. They were furious and humiliated. Any sign of cruelty towards the prisoners or hesitation in obeying his orders earned them a whipping from Dax, which he found surprisingly enjoyable.

Once the men had completed the cleanup, Dax arbitrarily divided the men into two groups and had one group kill the other, warning them that would be all of their fates if they didn't take better care of the prisoners, and the camp.

While all that was going on, Stryker stood by watching, showing no emotions, giving away nothing, keeping Dax in a state of worry that it hadn't been what Stryker had wanted.

It was only later, on their way back to camp, that Stryker finally spoke up, and Dax knew he had been spared for now. But not the camp. In three days, Stryker wanted the prison camp destroyed, with everyone in it.

Yes, it had been wrong to treat the prisoners that way, but he didn't want to waste any more resources on keeping the prisoners alive. They had been given a chance to convert to Aaron-Lem and had chosen not to.

This last part Dax knew wasn't correct. They had never been given a choice because they were too dangerous to Stryker and Aaron. Dax knew that Stryker was eliminating anyone that could oppose him and Aaron. That was something that Dax understood. Get rid of your enemies before they got rid of you.

What Stryker didn't know was that Dax was also his enemy. Not because he wanted to be all-powerful or a god. Dax had a much better reason. He had discovered what had happened to his village.

One day he might share that information with Ibris. Perhaps the two of them could temporarily be brothers again as they eliminated Stryker together.

But for now, he was happy to keep up the pretense while he figured out what Stryker was doing on the Island. Besides, Stryker knew something that Dax needed to find out. He was hoping that Stryker would lead him to it without resorting to torturing him, but if he had to, he would.

"Do you have any requests on how I destroy the camp?" Dax asked Stryker as they neared the Hetale village of Tiwa. They hadn't spoken more than a few words since Stryker had told Dax to kill the prisoners.

"Yes, make it look natural. No one needs to know that you were responsible for the death of every magical person on the Islands. How you do it is up to you, but it needs to happen three days from now."

Dax caught the meaning behind Stryker's words. If something went wrong, it wouldn't be Stryker people would blame. It would be Dax.

Thirty-Three

The cabin was small but dry, and that was all that they needed as the biggest and loudest storm Meg had ever experienced slapped Lopel. Tarek said after the storm they would build bunk beds around the inside perimeter of the cabin so everyone wasn't stepping over each other as they settled in for the night.

At first, Meg had trouble sleeping. She wasn't used to doing physical labor, and the little that she did that day made her arms and legs ache. That, and the shift to Ordinary every night, was forcing her to look more closely at her relationships. Or more precisely, her lack of them.

She knew that Ruth was right. She needed to adjust to being with people and learn how to work with them. And now that people surrounded her in a tiny space, she had no choice but to figure out how to get along with them.

She had never seen so many men in one place before and was having a hard time figuring out how to relate to all of them. Besides Leon and his crew of eight men, there was Roar and Tarek. That left her, Wren, Ruth, and Silke as the only women. Although Silke could fit in a pocket, so Meg wasn't sure if that counted.

The four women choose a corner of the cabin, hoping to stay out of the way of all the men stepping over each other. They managed to fall asleep together while the storm raged outside.

Once during the night, Meg woke and saw Tarek and Leon sitting close together whispering. Leon looked worried, but Tarek had the same quiet look that he always had. *Perhaps as a wizard, he has to look that way,* she thought and fell back to sleep. In spite of everything, it turned out to be the best sleep she had for longer than she could remember.

In Woald, she had been terrified every night and barely slept expecting someone to discover her at any moment, and she would have no powers to defend herself.

Back in Erda she was either playing or pranking, every night, not worrying about her future at all. In the cabin surrounded by men who could build a cabin in a day, a wizard, Silke the Okan, and three other shapeshifters, she felt protected.

Perhaps this is what her parents and sister had tried to provide for her, but she never let them. Would she now? Meg wondered. *Had she changed enough or would she revert to her wild ways?*

However, just before dawn, Meg woke herself up screaming, and in the process woke up everyone else who was still sleeping. Ruth was already awake and held Meg's hand as she tried to calm herself.

"What happened?" Tarek asked, squatting in front of her fixing his clear blue eyes on her.

"I don't know. That never happened before," Meg answered. "I was sleeping, and then I started hearing people yelling for me to help them. I tried to find out where the voices were coming from, but I couldn't see anything. Everything around me was black and wet. It was so wet. Then faces started floating by, and their mouths were open as if they were screaming." Meg shuttered, "It was awful. It felt so real."

Tarek rocked back on his heels staring at Meg. "So you have never had dreams like that before?"

When Meg shook her head, Tarek tilted his head at Leon and Silke, and the three of them stepped outside together. When they opened the door, the blue light of Etar filtered in, and the air smelled fresh and clean.

Meg was relieved. It was daylight again, she was back to being a shapeshifter, or she would be soon. Meg had noticed that it took longer every day for her powers to return. It scared her so much she couldn't think about it or tell anyone. It had to be her secret because becoming Ordinary more hours every day was the most frightening thing she could imagine.

Outside, Tarek and Leon walked to the lake, Silke resting on Leon's shoulder. There was destruction everywhere. Trees had tipped over in the punishing rain, and every plant they could see was plastered into the ground. The lake had flooded its banks leaving large mounds of debris on the shore as it had sunk back to its normal levels.

"Do you think her nightmare was because of the storm?" Leon asked.

Tarek looked at his cousin and asked, "Do you?"

Both of them turned back to watching the now calm lake reflect Trin as it rose above the horizon. There was no need to say anything more. They both knew that Meg had witnessed something that was going to happen. But what was it, and when?

The cabin was there for everyone's protection when they needed it, but they couldn't stay there and still save the Islands from the Kai-Via, or keep Aaron from destroying magic. They couldn't hide out at the lake hoping no one found them, or stay safe while more people died at the hands of Stryker and the men who obeyed him.

What they didn't know was why Stryker was even on the Islands. The Islands were small, and not necessary for world trade. There were no more Mages on the Island than anywhere else on Thamon. But for some reason, Stryker had decided to come himself, and send his most elite preacher and Kai-Via. Why?

They would have to venture back into the population to find the answers, and if Meg's nightmare told them anything, it was that something big was in the works.

"Do you think it has anything to do with the missing Mages?" Silke asked.

"I do," Wren said. Wren had come to join them after watching the three of them leave the cabin. "These are my Islands. I appreciate that you are here to help save them, but I think you should involve those of us who live here."

Tarek smiled at Wren. "You are absolutely right, Wren. Maybe you could fill us in on when and how they went missing. I'm sorry that I keep forgetting that you are not a young girl. You are much more than that, aren't you?"

"That's not important at the moment. Right now, let's find the missing people before it's too late," Wren replied. As she spoke, Wren knew that sooner or later, she would have to tell Tarek her story.

But she was going to put it off as long as possible. For now, they had some people to save from Aaron and his minions.

Thirty-Four

After hearing the story of how the Mages had slowly disappeared, the group discussed their next move. Leon and his men couldn't be seen by Stryker. Even though Stryker had barely paid attention to any of them on board the ship, that might have been a ruse, and he knew them all.

The group decided that Leon and his men would stay at the cabin. Tarek and Leon had always been able to communicate without being near each other, so when they found the missing people, Tarek would contact Leon, and he would know what to do. It made Meg wonder if Leon was really Ordinary.

"Being able to hear thoughts, and mind-speak is not magic, Meg, or not the way that Aaron-Lem describes it. Otherwise, their whole means of conversion would be deemed magic," Ruth said, reading Meg's thoughts.

"So if Leon and his men are not magic, how will they come to help?" Meg asked. "They're Ordinary. They can't fly or transport themselves there."

Meg ignored the angry faces on some of the men when she called them Ordinary.

"Meg," Ruth said, "You are judging these men, and you have already seen what they can do."

Meg huffed, "Okay, but still, I am telling the truth. They can't fly or transport themselves. What if we need them right away and they're across the island?"

"We?" Wren said. "Do you think you are coming with us?"

Meg transformed herself into a raven and then back to herself. "I can be anything or anyone. You need me."

"And at night, you are Ordinary. Just like what you call these men. If they can't do anything because they are Ordinary, then you can't either."

Tarek, who had been silently watching the exchange, held up his hand.

"Enough. This division between Mage and Ordinary is exactly what Stryker and Aaron are promoting. You are acting like them, making one of you more important than another. What is wrong with you? If any of you are going to do that, why not just go get yourself converted into Aaron-Lem and become part of the problem."

"That's a great idea," Roar said. "Let me do it. I'll convert to Aaron-Lem. It's just words. I've listened to the Preacher before. I know I can block his words in my head. No one will suspect me. To them, I am an old man. I don't even need to shapeshift to look old. I can let go of shapeshifting and look like myself."

With that, the younger version of Roar dissolved and he stood there as his true self. Older than he had been before.

"So you've been shapeshifting this whole time so you would appear younger?" Wren said, her hands on her hips.

"Aren't you doing the same thing, in your own way, Wren?" Seeing Wren's face, Roar backpedaled. "Sorry, I know it's not the same thing. For me, it was vanity. But since I am old, I am the perfect person to spy for you."

Wren stared at Roar for a full minute before replying. "You're right. It's not the same thing. And you're also right. You are the perfect person to do this. But it's more dangerous than just blocking his words. If he sees that you are blocking him, you'll probably disappear, too. That is, if you're lucky. If it's Stryker that notices, he won't bother to disappear you, he'll kill you instead."

"I know. But do you have a better suggestion?"

Tarek held up his hand again. "Agreed, you are the perfect person. But how will we communicate with you if you are going to stay away from Stryker's thought police?"

"I'll do it," Meg said. "I know you don't trust me, but I don't have anyone but you. Let me help. I can watch over Roar, and I'll get the information back to you."

One of Leon's men spoke up. "Let me go with Roar," he said. "We look a little alike. I can say he is my father and we can convert together. If Stryker recognizes me, I'll tell him Leon threw me overboard when he caught me stealing food, and I swam to shore. But he won't. I kept my face hidden from him."

Leon turned to his man and said, "Vald, are you sure?"

"I can alter his face a little," Ruth said.

"Can you do that for everyone?" Tarek asked.

"Yes, but not all at one time. I'm sorry. But I can keep Vald's face the same if I am within the same vicinity. Wren and I have been hiding since the Kai-Via arrived. My family is protected here on Lopel. I will do anything to keep them safe."

Tarek nodded. "I think altering his face is too dangerous. What if you aren't near him for some reason? We don't know where Dax will take him. Otherwise, I agree with the plan.

"And now that we have one, we need to leave now. Meg's nightmare may have something to do with the missing Mages, and if they are calling her for help, whatever Stryker is planning to do is probably soon.

"Do whatever you need to do to get ready. We'll meet back

here in thirty minutes. Meg, could you stay for a minute?"

Meg stood as still as possible as she watched everyone else head back to the cabin. Even Silke left with Leon, leaving her alone with Tarek. It astonished her that her legs were shaking. Was she afraid of him? Or was it something else?

Tarek turned to look at her, and she realized it was something else. She wanted to please him. Had she ever wanted to please anyone before? And why him? She didn't have any time to figure it out before Tarek spoke.

"Did you understand what I said about dividing people? It makes you no better than the Kai-Via. I am counting on you, Meg. Don't disappoint me. People's lives are at stake, including yours. If Stryker finds you, he will have no mercy. He hates shapeshifters more than any other kind of Mage. Do you understand?"

Meg nodded mutely. Tarek took one last look and walked away, leaving Meg standing on the shore not sure what she believed anymore, or who she was. A sob escaped her lips. What she would give to see her sister and parents again. But with all the magic she could do, there was no hope that she ever would. That was then, this was now, and she had to choose who she wanted to be.

"Perhaps wanting to please you is enough," Silke whispered into Tarek's ear, meeting him at the cabin door. He glanced back at Meg standing on the shore by herself. "Perhaps. But I think that she is going to need much more than that to stay alive and help us. Let's hope she finds it soon."

Thirty-Five

Thirty minutes later, they were all standing by the lake getting ready to go. The decision was made to use the deserted building that Meg had been staying in as their meeting place.

At the last minute, Ruth asked to come too. Even if she couldn't change Vald's face, she could help in other ways. No one said it out loud, but there was the worry that Meg would need help at night, or maybe even in the day. No one knew how Meg would behave working in a team. It was all new to her.

Besides, everyone knew how Ruth felt about Roar. She had to be there in case he needed help.

That left Leon and seven of his men back at the cabin. Meg didn't believe that they were going to be sitting around waiting. Something else had to be going on. But she decided to let it be, since no one was going to tell her anyway. She supposed that they still didn't trust her. *I'll prove them wrong*, Meg thought to herself.

By the time Wren, Meg, Ruth, and Roar reached the building, Tarek, Silke, and Vald were already waiting for them. Seeing them standing there waiting, Wren burst out laughing.

"Why didn't you tell us you could do that, Tarek? Here we had to shapeshift and travel across the island, and you could have just transported us. What else can you do that you aren't telling us?"

Looking at Meg standing with her arms crossed and a scowl on her face, Tarek asked, "Something bothering you, Meg?"

When she shook her head and turned away, Tarek winked at Wren and whispered, "More coming."

Wren laughed again, "Looking forward to it."

Meg watched everyone else enjoy the fact that Tarek could transport people, and felt left out. She sulked and turned away from the group and then realized that she was embarrassed that she was sulking.

Silke flew to Meg's shoulder and whispered, "You have to include yourself, Meg. No one is excluding you. You are the one who is doing it."

When a single tear rolled down Meg's cheek, embarrassing her even more, Silke added, "We need your help. Can you let go of this, and join the group? I think you can."

Meg nodded, wiped the tear off her face, and turned around. Everyone smiled at her, and to her amazement, Meg felt herself smile back. Perhaps she could do this after all.

****

As they walked across the Arrow on their way to the Temple on Hetale, Roar and Vald overheard everyone talking about the storm. The people of the Islands were used to storms, but these new storms were different, and this last one was especially brutal.

Although all the stalls and tents had been dismantled before the storm hit, saving them from the wave that washed over the Arrow, the destruction was evident. All the vegetation was gone. And as the tents went up for the day, it seemed as if there was less room between them and the roadway than before.

Roar and Vald noticed that one man was doing a lot of complaining, and his neighbors were doing their best to shush him, looking around to see who had noticed what he was saying. The man kept claiming it was because the Kai-Via had come to the Islands and taken away all the Mages who had held the storms in check.

Roar knew the other vendors were trying to protect him, and at the same time not draw attention to themselves. If anyone from the Kai-Via, or any of their zealots, heard his complaining he would put himself and everyone around him in danger.

No one was allowed to speak against the Kai-Via or Aaron. People disappeared who disagreed with the Aaron-Lem doctrines.

Roar made a small motion with his hand, and the man suddenly stopped talking. Relieved, everyone went back to putting up their tents and stalls.

Roar and Vald walked over to the now silent man to help put up his tent. Quietly, Roar said, "You have to be careful, my friend, you never know who is listening. Is it true that the storms are getting worse? We are new to these Islands and didn't know that you had Mages that helped control the weather."

The man whispered back, "We did. And now we don't. Something is wrong. Every time that Preacher talks, people fall for whatever he is saying, and then they go get themselves converted, and they aren't the same after that."

"How are they different?" Vald asked, hoisting up the back of the tent and setting it in place.

"Well, for one thing, you can't have a normal conversation anymore. The Kai-Via either try to get me to shut up or convert me to that one true God nonsense. Aaron is not my God, and never will be."

"So you don't feel different after the Preacher talks?" Roar asked.

"The only thing I feel is angry. I lose more friends every time he comes here."

Vald took the man's arm and moved close to him. "Be careful. If they notice his words don't affect you, you could be one of the ones that disappear. If you want to help, there are better ways than talking too much."

The man nodded, extended his hand, and introduced himself as Samis. "There are others like me, but I guess they know better, they keep quiet."

"Do you think you could gather them?"

When Samis nodded yes, Vald added, "Be sure none of them are faking it, Samis, because otherwise all of you will be a risk. When you are sure, hang a blue cloth at your table, and we'll stop by and tell you where to meet us."

"Are you going to stop them?" Samis asked.

"That's the plan," Roar said. "But we need information. If you and your people can gather it, we will be one step ahead."

Samis nodded. "Understood."

Roar turned to go and then came back, "Not only keep quiet but also look converted. Keep your mind and your mouth closed. Do you understand?"

As Roar and Vald walked away, Vald asked, "Is he for real? Do you think we can trust him?"

"I don't know," Roar said. "I didn't feel anything off about him, but if he is good, he could be projecting what we wanted to see, and blocking the rest."

Both of them walked the rest of the way to the Temple in silence, hoping that they could do what needed to be done still aware that they could be walking into a trap. But it was the best plan that they had, for now.

Thirty-Six

The ocean was lapping gently against the shore, providing a soothing background to Stryker's thoughts. The only sign of last night's storm was the debris lying on the beach.

Etar and Trin were almost at their midpoint crossing, and Stryker had walked down the steps carved into the cliffs to watch for the blue flash. He knew that people considered it a good omen if they saw it, and there was no reason for him to not accept that as true. It wasn't magic. It was superstition.

There was one thing that Stryker knew, without a doubt. Whatever someone believed had more power than truth. Whatever the truth was, since it was all relative to the person believing it.

So accepting good fortune because of a blue flash was a wise thing to do. It would set up his unconscious mind to make sure that it happened that way. It was why he didn't let negative ideas invade his thinking, and banished anyone or anything that could influence his thoughts away from what he wanted.

The inequality of what he enforced wasn't lost on Stryker. He didn't let anyone change, or impact, his belief, and thoughts, but he intentionally forced his desires into the minds of others. It was so much easier than people thought.

Obviously, he chuckled to himself. *Look what Aaron and I have done together with it.*

The power of the subconscious to provide what people believed, wanted to believe, allowed themselves to believe, had enabled Stryker and Aaron to rule Thamon.

He and Aaron had been planning the takeover of Thamon for their entire lives. They had met as children in school. Both of them were bored and did things they weren't supposed to do just to make the day more interesting.

At first, they were enemies. They both loved being the one that caused disruption and chaos in the classrooms and didn't like someone else doing it too.

It was Aaron who called the truce. "Why work against each other?" he had asked. "Let's work together. Imagine what it would be like to be the rulers of this classroom, then the school, and then the town?"

And there it was. The beginning of what would work for them for the rest of their lives. The power of imagination. Aaron painted a picture of what that would feel like, what they could do, how people would honor and worship them. He filled Stryker's mind with the images of being all-powerful, and then once he had Stryker's attention, Aaron told them how they would do it.

Aaron had the advantage of a focused one-track mind, while Stryker would see, and try, multiple ways to accomplish what they wanted to do. Together they were a force no one could stop.

They perfected their techniques of subconscious and conscious suggestion. They tested it over and over again, noticing who fell for it immediately, and who didn't.

It didn't take long before it became glaringly apparent that the Mages were not affected by their suggestions. Aaron was the first Preacher for Aaron-Lem. His focus, attention, and his words both spoken and unspoken attached themselves with tiny tendrils into minds and didn't let go, producing a desire to follow and believe whatever he said.

But the Mages would listen, apparently entranced, but did not choose to believe it without trying out the truth of what was said. And it was the beliefs and words embedded into their subconscious that made people his followers, and that meant the Mages were not.

Aaron and Stryker knew from the beginning that designing a new religion was necessary to give structure to their process of converting the people to their rule. It wasn't really a conversion, it was submission, but that wasn't something they said.

Conversion was something people understood. They wanted an all-powerful God that would guide them in times of trouble and bring them into the promised land that Aaron promised them.

Stryker and Aaron tried out a variety of names for their new religion. In the end, they choose the obvious, Aaron-Lem. It made the most sense because they wanted the people to believe that Aaron was the one true God. To the people of Thamon, the word Lem meant a warrior god. It was the perfect name.

At first, Aaron and Stryker let the Mages alone, not sure how to control them anyway. Instead, they focused on getting better at converting people, finding more effective ways to bait the hook and reel the people into Aaron-Lem.

For a long time, the Mages didn't try to stop the spread of Aaron-Lem. However, as time went by, the Mages began to protest as people stopped thinking for themselves and instead accepted whatever Aaron-Lem told them to think and do.

Once the Mages discovered that when Aaron-Lem's mental conversions didn't work, violence was used, they started speaking out. And that's when Aaron and Stryker decided to eliminate magic. If they couldn't control it, it couldn't exist.

And for the most part, they had been successful. Mages had either died or been imprisoned as Aaron and Stryker used them to find out why they couldn't convert them. Many Mages were killed in the process.

As the blue light flashed overhead, Stryker thought about the problem he had given himself. He had given Dax three days to destroy the camp. He had wanted to force Dax's hand.

But by doing so, he had given himself only a few days to discover and retrieve what he had come to the Islands for, and then leave before the destruction, thereby avoiding any reference to himself. He could have used more time, but now that he had said it, how could he go back on it?

As Stryker listened to the waves lapping on the shore, he knew what he could do. He could tell Dax that Aaron spoke to him and asked to have the camp spared for a few more days.

Ha, Stryker thought to himself. *As if.* Aaron was too busy ruling an entire planet to care anything at all about these Islands.

As far as Aaron was concerned, the conversion of the people of Thamon had been a total success. He had everyone doing exactly what he wanted them to, which consisted of making him more prosperous and powerful every day.

Aaron would have no compassion for the people in the camp. He would have had them destroyed immediately so that no resources, as meager as they were, were used to care for them.

Although it had been Stryker and his Preachers and bands of Kai-Via who had done the conversion, usually violently, Aaron was the one who had ordered it done.

If Aaron knew that Stryker was letting Ibris convert Lopel and Hetale as peacefully as possible, he would be furious. But he didn't know, and Stryker was going to keep it that way.

After he recovered what the map had shown him, he would let Dax take over, and do what he wanted with the people.

Ibris was another story, and he hadn't decided on the ending for that one yet.

Thirty-Seven

Ibris stood alone at the east wall of the temple looking towards Lopel. In the distance, he could see the curve of the shore and the blue-green ocean softly lapping onto the sand. He watched the white shorebirds flashing out of nowhere and diving into the waters to rise with a fish in their mouths.

Although he had been on the Islands only for a short time, he had begun to fall in love with their beauty and the rhythm of nature that thrived on them. It was simple, uncomplicated, and not like his life at all.

In a few hours, he would be expected to preach, and he was tired and didn't know how he would find the energy to do what he had to do. The blue light had flashed, and for a moment, he felt a little better. But knowing that what he would say would turn more people of these islands into his puppets bothered him.

And he couldn't let himself be bothered. He was the Preacher. He was in charge of the Kai-Via on these Islands. He was supposed to convert the people to Aaron-Lem, turning them into docile sheep that didn't question, but worked for Aaron.

It worried Ibris that Stryker was supporting the peaceful

conversion of the Islands. He had never known Stryker to be kind or patient, and yet he was acting as if he was. Something else had to be happening. Stryker was much too calm.

It probably had to do with the real reason he had come to the Islands, and that in itself was troubling. What if he found what he was looking for?

On the other hand, Dax had returned from his trip with Stryker full of fury and anxiety. Ibris knew that they had visited the prison camp where they kept the Mages and their families. He had asked to go with them. But Stryker had told him to stay behind. Someone needed to be in charge while they were gone.

That may have been true, but Ibris knew that it was more than that. They hadn't wanted him to see where the camp was located or how they were treating the prisoners. That Dax had been keeping it from him had been evident from the start.

Using the excuse that Ibris was too essential to be dealing with prisoners, Dax had continually thwarted him in finding the camp. Dax assured him that the prisoners were well cared for and that once they figured out how to convert them they would be released.

Ibris didn't believe any of that for a moment. Yes, there had been a time when he would have convinced himself that Dax was telling the truth. He had loved Dax. Being thrown together after both their families had died had created a bond that Ibris thought could never be broken. And yet it was.

Now they were pitted against each other even though both of them pretended to still be friends. Friends that didn't talk and didn't trust each other.

Ibris knew they weren't friends anymore, let alone spirit brothers as they had once called themselves. He and Dax were no longer on the same path. Although Stryker had trained them both, Dax became a warrior, and he became a Preacher.

Truthfully, Ibris knew that he was a liar and a coward. He preached for a tyrant because he was afraid. He continued to preach and convert because he had no idea how not to. He couldn't rise up against Aaron, Stryker, and now Dax. He had no way to stop them. He couldn't run. They would find him.

All he could do was try to keep the people content so they wouldn't be locked up or killed. It was an act of rebellion so small, it meant nothing.

Ibris lowered himself to his knees. It was that time of day. Bow to Aaron. He knew that all over Thamon people were bowing to Aaron. How many of them, he wondered, were like him, bowing because they didn't know what else to do.

****

Roar and Vald waited patiently with the rest of the crowd for the Preacher to arrive. The Temple walls were open, and a light breeze carrying the scent of flowers ruffled the panels that had been pulled back to reveal the view.

In the distance were the cliffs of Lopel and the ocean. Close by was a lovely garden, filled with paths to walk, and benches to use for quiet meditation. *Whoever had designed the Temple and the gardens knew how beauty refreshed the spirit*, Roar thought to himself.

Inside, the Temple was equally serene. It was a vast off-white open space that somehow still felt intimate. Sprigs of native flowers in huge vases sat in front of every column that upheld the round roof. Since this was not a conversion ceremony, the pool wasn't in the middle of the floor. Instead, there were rows of whitewashed wood benches, filled with people of all ages.

First, the Seven Kai-Via entered the Temple and stood against the north wall looking out over the gathering. Then a low hum began. It was a melody so soft that Roar wasn't sure if it was actually there or if he imagined it.

It was the first time he had come to hear the Preacher at the Temple, and as the melody flowed through him, Roar began to understand how easy it would be to float along with it and let go.

At the same time, Roar felt Vald tense up, as if he was resisting the hum, and when Roar noticed that Vald was clenching his fist, he understood that Vald was afraid.

He leaned in and softly whispered, "Don't worry, it won't affect me. I'll keep you safe." Vald nodded but didn't look any less afraid. "Stop it Vald. You are going to stand out doing that. Do you want me to help?"

Vald didn't say anything, but the look on his face gave Roar the answer. He whispered a few words, and Vald sighed and stopped clenching his fist. Roar wasn't so sure that Vald would like what he just did when he found out, but it would be better than having the Preacher do it to him. Besides, he would wake him out of it when the meeting was over.

The hum faded about the same time that the Preacher glided to the front of the stage. A figure in a black robe stood alone in front of the Seven. He could have been anyone. Except as soon as he spoke the first words, it was apparent that this was the famous Preacher.

His words were like a gentle mist that filled the room, bringing with it a sense of peace and happiness. Roar let himself sink into the words, feeling what everyone was feeling.

It was lovely, and Roar wanted it never to end.

Thirty-Eight

Aaron was in the middle of designing new rituals for Aaron-Lem when he felt something that he used to call fear, but now he called an Alert. He could never show fear, ever. He was God.

At the time Aaron felt the Alert, he was in the middle of directing his staff for the day. He wasn't fooling himself by calling the people that served him his staff. He knew they were prisoners. Not the kind that are locked up in a prison camp where he kept the Mages before eliminating them.

These were his emotional prisoners. They would do anything for him because they had no choice. Their minds were his.

But it was always good to add more layers to their mental prison. Besides, Aaron loved the beauty of rituals. Watching the converts walk into the ceremonial pools always struck a chord of harmony in his heart.

When he was the only Preacher of Aaron-Lem, Aaron had witnessed many conversion ceremonies, and the power and beauty of them would carry him to new heights of joy and motivate him to create more rituals, and convert more people.

Of course, it had been a brilliant move on his part to make sure that all of the Kai-Via and Preachers wore black robes. At the time, it was because he didn't want a human form to represent their God. It was only later when he wanted to secretly watch his people bow to him three times a day, that he was glad they had no idea what he looked like under the robes.

Even now, no one knew, except Stryker. If anyone had remembered Aaron from his youth, they wouldn't know him now. He had made sure of that. That left the people who worked for him. But they didn't know what he looked like either. Not because he was wearing his black robe, but because they were blind.

He loved that double meaning. Yes, they were blind. Blind to what he had done to their belief systems so that they were prisoners of Aaron-Lem. But they were also physically blind.

That was another of his rituals. Only the best converts could serve the one true God. He had instilled in them the belief that if they saw him, even in his human form, it would kill them. So if they had achieved the honor of serving him in his home, they had to be willing to go through the blinding ceremony.

It wasn't as bad as it sounded. He wasn't a monster. It was fairly painless. A momentary discomfort as a few drops of oil from a plant they grew just for that purpose were dropped into each of the Blessed One's eyes. Yes, the Blessed Ones. Not slaves. Not prisoners. Blessed Ones. He even had a waiting list of people willing to serve him and be blinded for the pleasure.

Because although they couldn't see him, they could hear him. They knew that only they would have the honor of receiving his blessing every day. They would shiver in joy and speak of his glory as he spoke. It was Aaron's daily drug, watching their reactions to what he was doing to them.

His voice moved through them like a laser, locking into every emotion and thought, and binding them more tightly into the service of Aaron-Lem.

The only downside was they had to be trained to serve

him as a blind person. He had a building set aside just for that reason. It was a school for the recently blind, taught by other staff, but not the ones that served him directly.

If he needed to speak to the schools' faculty, he wore his black robes. Many of that staff begged to be blinded, to come into his home, but he rarely granted that request. They were too valuable to him as teachers.

Once each Blessed One completed the training, their reward was one-on-one with their God, Aaron.

With all those incentives, Aaron thought, *who wouldn't choose that?* To be so close to God that you heard him every day, His voice always close by. There was no need to search for what God wanted you to do.

As God, Aaron told them what to think, what to do, and how to behave. There was no more confusion about what was right or wrong. Just follow Aaron's voice. Life was simple. Serve Aaron, and happiness was the result.

There were two classes of Blessed Ones, and they each served Aaron differently. The men took care of his business needs, followed his orders, prepared his meals, and kept his home maintained.

The women had it easier, or so Aaron believed. They were pampered and cared for by the men. They had nothing to do except wait for Aaron to choose them for his other needs.

If they didn't please him, they died. It was that simple. Once again, there was no confusion. But not satisfying Aaron rarely happened, because they wanted to serve their God. But he brooked no deviance from their submission to him.

He did not allow women to serve in any other way or have any power. Even when they were not Mages, women had some kind of magic that made him afraid, But that was his secret. His and Stryker's.

Thinking about Stryker brought Aaron back to the Alert he had felt earlier. It had something to do with Stryker. Even though he and Stryker were friends and business partners in the building of Aaron-Lem, he always kept his spies watching for what Stryker was doing. He did this even though he was grateful for Stryker. Without him, he could never have ruled Thamon.

Stryker had followed his direction and destroyed cities and villages whenever Aaron requested it. Sometimes Stryker had asked if he could destroy them differently because he wanted to see if it would work. And of course, Aaron had always agreed. "Just get it done," he would say to him. And Stryker did.

But what was Stryker doing now? Aaron wondered. Aaron reached out with his mind and called to the man overseeing his spies, and told him that he needed to see him immediately. Then he told the man who was standing patiently on the side of the room waiting for orders to get him his black robe. It was time to find out where Stryker was and what he was doing. Something was off. He needed to find out what it was.

Speaking to others in their minds was not magic. It was a skill. But it was a skill that only he and his Preachers were allowed to use. And Stryker. Which brought him back to wondering what Stryker was doing? Why did he feel that Alert?

Putting aside his latest plans for a new ritual, Aaron donned his black robe and clapped his hands. He was ready to find out what was going on.

Thirty-Nine

After making sure that everyone was settled back in Woald, Tarek and Silke returned to the cave. They could have arrived inside the cave, but instead chose to walk down to it, enjoying the beauty that surrounded and hid the cave.

Tarek and Silke arrived on the barely visible path to the cave that curved through the forest. Large evergreen and deciduous trees stood side by side, protecting the opening from prying eyes, and shading the path. With Silke sitting on his shoulder, Tarek followed the trail as it curved around until it reached the hill above the cave.

Below them, a mist almost blocked the view to the cave opening. The coolness of the water from the cave reacted with the warmer outside air of the forest that protected it, and the resulting fog made the cave look even more mysterious and magical.

Tarek walked down the steps carved into the hillside while Silke flew ahead of them to the waiting rowboat. Tarek knew that Leon had made sure there was always a boat waiting for him at the opening and he sent out a 'thank you' to Leon. He knew that Leon would receive it and smile because Tarek was on his way.

Instead of using magic to move the boat along, Tarek rowed, enjoying the feeling of being one with the rowboat. He didn't turn on the lights or heat that he had set up for everyone else. Tarek liked feeling as if he had stepped into another world.

It was so dark in the cave that if he hadn't placed a ball of light in the bow of the boat, they wouldn't have been able to see their hands in front of their faces. He sent out lights that flew in front of them so they could see the sides and crevices of the cave.

It hadn't taken Tarek long to discover some of the mysteries of the cave. There were deep openings hidden behind the massive stalactites that had formed after thousands of years of water seeping through the ceiling. When Silke had first asked him how old the cave was, Tarek answered that it was over three hundred and fifty million years old. Not something easy to contemplate, even for a wizard or an Okan, Silke's heritage.

Okans lived for hundreds of years, serving and guiding the wizards that they had been bonded with for their lifetime. Tarek was Silke's third wizard in his line. His father and grandfather had been under her care. Having an Okan that had served two wizards before him was an honor for Tarek. There weren't many of her race, and having one like Silke was an even greater honor, one that he hoped he would be able to live up to.

Silke knew more than he could ever know about life, magic, and the complications of relationships. Tarek was aware that Silke might choose to move through the next door, called death, with him, instead of staying on. But that would depend on if he ever had an heir that she could, or wanted to, bond with to remain on Thamon.

So far in his life, Tarek had never felt a need to marry, or bond with any woman. He was young in wizard years, so he knew there was time, and if it were meant to be, it would be.

But nobody had ever caught his eye, let alone any piece of his heart, and he had been perfectly happy with that.

As he drifted through the cave, mapping in his mind every turn and corner, he let a piece of his mind rest on Meg. She was a curious one. On the surface, he shouldn't like her, let alone trust her. She was selfish and untrained.

But there was something that pulled him in her direction. Tarek didn't think it was just because he felt a nudge of compassion for her, having found herself on a strange planet where the ruling powers hated her kind.

There was a possibility that there was more to Meg, and if so, perhaps more to the pull he felt towards her. Silke, aware of both his heart and his thinking, flew back to his shoulder and kissed him on the cheek before heading out again on her own.

Tarek knew that was her way of saying that she agreed. Meg might turn out to be the one that he would bond with, but she was far from capable at the moment. So at least for now their relationship would remain a teacher to student. He wasn't even sure Meg wanted that relationship.

As the boat slipped through a narrow opening, Tarek ducked to keep from hitting the large ledge that jutted out across the water. Looking closely, he saw the massive cavern behind it that he had discovered while looking for the perfect place to hide. The cavern was big enough for their purposes, and it had a natural step up from a boat to the ledge.

The cave was a constant temperature year-round, although the Islands could get very hot during the warm season and very cold in the cold months. Tarek was sure that other peoples had used this cave and these caverns for protection from the elements and other dangers throughout the ages. He would need to return and make peace with any of them still resting there before they used it.

The spirits of those who hadn't entirely made it through the door to the next life could either be helpful or harmful. Tarek's task would be to help complete the journey for those who hadn't realized that the light was waiting for them, or make peace with those who were choosing to stay for their own reasons.

But this wasn't the time. They had a few more things to put into motion. As the boat made the next turn, the sunlight from the end of the cave streamed in, and Tarek let the light that he was producing dim out. Tarek caught sight of Silke visiting one of the birds nesting on the ledges and little openings that existed at the mouth of the cave.

She was sitting on one of the ledges swinging her legs and chirping back at the tiny bird sitting on her nest. Silke could have passed for a bird at that moment if her legs didn't look so human. Catching his thoughts, she smiled and created the illusion of bird legs for him.

Then she said, "No one has been here for centuries beside us, Tarek." Nodding towards the small gray bird beside her, Silke added, "She says this will be a safe place for what you are planning."

As the lake came into view, Tarek let himself be filled with its beauty. Ducks came close to the boat, deer were standing at the edge of the lake drinking, and he could hear the song of hundreds of birds weaving their way through the trees that surrounded the lake. Although he couldn't see the cabin, he saw a plume of smoke rising through the trees. By the time it hit the top of the tree line, it had dissolved. They didn't want to be discovered by something as simple as smoke in the distance.

However, Tarek knew that the smoke meant that Leon was cooking. His mouth watered as he moved the boat quickly to the shore. Food first, then they could put the next part of the plan into action.

Forty

Dax couldn't decide if Stryker giving him more time to destroy the prison camp bothered him or not. *What if Stryker had a sinister plan behind the change of mind?* Stryker had said that Aaron told him to delay the destruction, but Dax didn't believe that for a moment. It was something that Stryker wanted. But perhaps he could use it to his advantage.

It gave him time to design a plan that would give him the most pleasure. Rather than rush through it, he could make it spectacular. Much more fun. Stryker said that he didn't care anymore if it looked natural. Just get rid of the prison.

But that didn't mean Dax couldn't do it in the way they had originally planned. What if an entirely "natural" event did take place? So natural Stryker couldn't figure out if Dax had done it or not?

As Dax pondered these ideas, he was grateful for the black robes he was wearing. It was so freeing! Standing behind Ibris as Ibris used words to weave his spell, Dax could plan.

The Temple was packed. People were standing outside the Temple walls ten layers deep hoping to catch a glimpse of what was going on inside, and hear the Preacher's words. What they didn't know was that they didn't have to hear the words to get the message. While he spoke, Ibris was also broadcasting the underlying message into their subconscious minds.

It was how they caught the Mages. Neither the spoken or unspoken words would take hold. Dax knew that some of them pretended that they did, but it never worked. The Seven had been trained to spot anyone whose mind appeared to be open but was actually closed.

Dax thought of the other six men by his side. Even though they worked together as the Kai-Via, they rarely spoke to each other except to complete their tasks. Their job was to convert the people and eliminate those who couldn't or wouldn't choose Aaron-Lem.

They were each chosen separately, handpicked by Stryker. Sometimes he replaced one of the Seven without any notice. Friendship among the Kai-Via was actively discouraged. Dax knew that there were multiple Kai-Via teams, but they never met each other. He suspected they were all like his Kai-Via. One of them would be the aggressor, and the others followed orders. Not his orders. The Preacher's orders. However, they all knew that Stryker and then Aaron overrode any Preacher.

There were rumors that some Preachers had rebelled against Aaron-Lem. It was bound to happen. They had been trained to keep their minds closed, so others couldn't influence them. But Dax was sure some of them closed their minds to Stryker and Aaron, too, and managed to hide it. Like Ibris.

Dax didn't trust him, even though they had once been so close. Ibris had given Dax no reason to doubt his motives. It was just a feeling that he had. He knew that Ibris didn't trust him, either. Sooner or later, something would happen to disrupt the seemingly perfect process they had in place. Dax was looking forward to it. In fact, if he had a chance, he would be the one that started it.

However, at the moment, he wanted to have fun destroying the camp. He couldn't ask any of the six to help him. That would be going against orders, and they might report him to keep in the good graces of Stryker. Half of the men he had trained to help him capture Mages, were now dead after the debacle at the prison camp.

Dax almost laughed out loud at that thought, smothering it at the last minute. Kai-Via never moved during sermons, let alone showed any emotion. Standing as still as statues, in their black robes, with only shadowy eyes and mouths showing, they were the symbol of a threat.

It amazed Dax how few people consciously understood what they were doing. Unconsciously, they all did. And that as much as the Preacher's words and Aaron's rituals, caused conversions.

No, he would have to find someone else to help with the camp. Someone who could easily cause a natural disaster. Like a Mage. He suspected that there were at least three in the crowd right now. One of them was doing an excellent job of looking as if he was falling into the Preacher's spell. The other two felt different.

Oh, that would be great, Dax thought to himself as he noticed two ravens sitting in a tree nearby. He had seen them before. What if they were the other two, it would be perfect. Aaron and Stryker hated shapeshifters more than any other kind of Mage.

For a good reason. They could be anyone. Or in this case, anything. If Dax was right, and he thought that he was, he needed to find a way to trap them. He could start with the Mage in the audience. The problem was it was hard to track which mind belonged to which person. This Mage appeared to be an expert at looking as if he was converting. None of his facial expressions were giving him away.

Then Dax noticed a large man sitting beside an older one, looking like father and son. The large one, the son, was clenching his fists. While Dax watched, something happened, and all the tension drained out of him, and his fists unclenched. *Yes, it was possible.* One of them was a Mage. Probably the older one. It was his lucky day. Two shapeshifters and a Mage, and who knew who that big guy was. He could be dangerous. Although looking at him, he appeared to be falling under the spell of the words. Maybe he was wrong. Perhaps they were Ordinaries, but something in the way the older man sat made Dax think he was right.

His eyes flicked up to where he had seen the ravens. They were gone. But if he were right about who and what they were, they would be back. Perhaps he could use the old man as a trap for them. Three Mages could easily produce a natural disaster. Dax was thinking of something like an earthquake. He wanted something that would quickly bury all the Mages and their families along with the camp.

Dax knew he was playing with fire. He might be able to capture those three, but could he control them? He would need help. He thought he knew which of his men would be perfect. Ibris would be preaching in the morning again, and he was betting that those three would be back. And he would be ready for them.

Forty-One

When the service was over, a loud sigh went out from the crowd. The converted wanted it to go on forever, and the newly interested wanted more.

What none of the people knew, and probably wouldn't have cared, was that the Preacher's words were a drug. It hit the part of their brain that made them feel good, and they wanted more. They would be back to get that feeling again. The Preacher was now holding two meetings a day. It still didn't seem as if it was enough to satisfy the need of the people.

Roar leaned against Vald, making it look as if he needed Vald's assistance to stand, but it was Vald who needed help. Vald shuddered as Roar moved through his mind, untangling some of the threads that had started to tangle themselves into his thinking.

Roar shut off the pleasure response in Vald's brain, apologizing as he did so, knowing how painful it could be after succumbing to the Preachers' words.

They shuffled out with the crowd, Roar doing his best to look as if Vald was supporting him, rather than the other way around. By the time they reached the Arrow, Vald had mostly returned to himself.

As agreed beforehand, they stopped at the Market to get food. They took it over to a table to watch the people passing through the market place, and to wait until someone told them where to go next.

"I'm afraid," Vald said, as they finished the last of their food. When Roar didn't say anything, Vald added, "I loved it. Everything he said, I loved. I wanted to feel that wonderful all the time."

Waiting for a beat, and lowering his voice until Roar could barely hear, he added, "And I still do."

Roar nodded and took a sip of his drink, but didn't reply. He understood what Vald was telling him, but this was not the time to discuss it. And he was afraid too. Not for the same reason, though.

It was Wren who came to the table and told them Tarek was waiting for them back at the building. Vald had been startled when a bird landed on his hand and started pecking on his roll, hopping down to the table to eat some of Roar's salad. To Vald, she looked like every other wren on the Islands if just a bit braver than most of them.

It was only when Roar stood, and the bird flew off, that Vald had an idea that it had been the actual Wren who had landed on his hand. It was a strange feeling to be around people who could do such things.

He had grown up in a house of what he heard Meg call Ordinaries. He didn't understand why she thought Ordinaries were less than her and her Mage friends. Why would they be? It was a different set of skills. Magical and Ordinary had never appeared as a divider before between him or anyone else. Or perhaps it was because most of his friends had been like him.

This magical, wizard, shapeshifter thing was disconcerting. And now the Preacher's words were still stuck in his head. He could feel them circling the door that Roar had closed for him, but he wanted more than anything to open the door and let the words back into his mind. Yes, he was afraid.

It took them an hour to make their way back to the building, a building that was only ten minutes away. But they wanted to be sure that no one had followed them. They stopped by Samis' tent and bought fruit from him, whispering that they would check back the next day.

They circled through the tents, and then once across the Arrow, they took the long way into Woald. In Woald, they turned corner after corner, and when they were sure that no one was following them, they headed to the deserted building.

Everyone was already there, milling around, chatting, waiting, and looking like their true selves. It pleased Vald that they let him see who they were. This new group of friends was beginning to feel like a crew on a ship. There was no room for pretense on the seas. They all had to work together, especially on that last voyage with Stryker on board. His presence put everyone on edge, afraid that he would turn on one of them, and they would disappear like so many of their friends.

Now Vald was part of this new crew, and he didn't want to let them down. So when Tarek asked him how it went at the Temple, he told the truth. He had been ready and willing to follow Aaron-Lem forever. If Roar had not been there, he would have signed up for the next conversion ceremony.

To his surprise, no one was upset. Instead, Ruth and Wren hugged him, and Tarek smiled.

"It's understandable, Vald. Ibris has become a master at using words to leash people's minds. Do you remember anything at all?"

"Besides Roar telling me it was okay, I don't remember the words as much as the feeling of happiness and joy and lack of worry. Fear of the future was gone. Fear, in general, was gone.

"All I remember hearing were the words, 'Imagine yourself …' and then strings of words describing something. Couldn't tell you what, though."

Tarek nodded. He knew how Ibris was doing what he was doing. He always began with the powerful words, "Imagine yourself," as the key to open the door to people's minds. Sometimes the exact words were used, and sometimes they were implied. Sometimes they were spoken out loud, and sometimes Ibris and the Kai-Via projected them to the subconscious.

Imagination is one of the most potent tools for transformation, and as with any tool, it can be used for both good or evil. Aaron and Stryker had chosen to use it for evil, and Ibris was the master for accomplishing it. Along with more of his subversive tricks, Ibris would be able to take over any open mind, willing or not.

But Tarek didn't say any of that to Roar. Instead, he asked Meg what she had learned, and she was startled by the question.

They were sitting in a circle on the floor of the building. Ruth had laid down blankets and cushions that she had found somewhere, making it relatively comfortable. Vald and Roar leaned up against one of the walls while everyone else sat with crossed legs or leaned back on piles of cushions.

Meg looked at each of them and then back to Tarek. She took a deep breath and said, "I learned that one of the Kai-Via knows who we are."

Forty-Two

Roar nodded. "Yes, Meg is right. Someone knew that Mages were there, and I think that whoever it was figured out that one of them was me. I am not sure about Meg and Ruth, though."

Tarek looked at Meg, and she nodded, "He knew who we were, or at least suspected.

"Ruth and I can't show up as ravens anymore. We might be able to try something else, but I'm sure that person knew we were shifters. But that's not all. He wanted us for something."

"Yes, to disappear us," Roar said bitterly, his face looking like his name.

"No. I don't think so. There is something else going on. I am not saying that he wants us for something good, but it's less like disappearing us and more like using us."

"If that's true, we need to find out what he wants us for," Wren said.

"Oh sure, we'll just volunteer to help out his evil plan. And who are we talking about anyway?" Ruth said. "You said one of the Kai-Via, so you don't mean the Preacher?"

Meg shook her head. "How can you tell? They are all lined up back there like black statues, nothing moving. Their eyes barely flicker. I'm not sure they even blink. At least on the

Preacher, you can see his lips move. So no, I don't know which one. Just someone. Does it matter who? We are in trouble no matter who it is."

Tarek had watched the discussion without saying anything, waiting to see where the debate would go. He was pleased to see that Meg had felt something. That could only happen if she were listening and open to being of service to someone other than herself. It was a good sign, so when she answered, he couldn't help but smile at her.

"Great observations, Meg and Roar. Yes, it's almost impossible to tell the Kai-Via apart. The Seven are meant to be anonymous, but I know that Stryker sent his best Kai-Via team and Preacher to the Islands, so I know who they are.

"That's not good news because that means that the aggressor in the Seven is Dax. Dax is ruthless and brilliant. He and the Preacher, whose name is Ibris, were trained together by Stryker himself, which makes them both the best that there is."

"So they both are the most ruthless?" Roar asked.

"Good question. That answer is, I doubt it. They were trained for different purposes. Ibris was trained in the skill of mental manipulation. He's better at it than anyone, including Stryker and Aaron, which I am sure scares them and someday will do something about it. However, it doesn't make him ruthless like Dax, who was trained in violence.

"The fact that Ibris is the best at conversion is a good reason not to beat yourself up, Vald. Besides, we might be able to use the fact that you are so susceptible.

"But since Dax knows that you are here, we have to be careful. And we need to find out what he wants to use you for, or me, if he knew I was here."

Tarek turned back to Meg, "So you think he knows about you and Ruth and Vald and Roar?"

"I think so. The good news is, I think Dax can only feel for Mages from a short distance, and Wren was in the market place, and you and Silke were here, I guess. So he doesn't know about you."

Tarek didn't answer Meg's thinly veiled question. Instead, he turned to Wren. "What did you learn?"

"Vald and Roar met a man named Samis, who is gathering a few people who are not converted and want to stop the Kai-Via. Not sure why the Preacher's words don't affect them, but I watched him, and he wasn't faking it. He gathered three men and one woman, and put out the blue cloth in his tent. He's ready when we are."

"What we first need from him is information, about what Dax may be up to," Tarek said. "My guess is that it is about the Mages who are missing from the Islands. Wren, if you could find out if he knows how many are gone, and where they took them, that would be the first step."

"You think this is all about the disappeared?" Silke asked. She had been quietly listening, sitting on Tarek's knee watching each member of the circle as they spoke.

Tarek nodded. "I do. And I think Stryker is letting him do whatever he wants because he wants Dax distracted while he does something else. Stryker has a map. He's searching for something. And it's something we can't let him find."

Everyone but Silke looked at Tarek in surprise. It was Wren who said, "And when were you going to tell us about it, Tarek?"

"I'm telling you now. We need to find out what Dax is up to, and still keep an eye on what Stryker is doing. Any ideas of how we can do this?"

"I can let Ibris convert me," Vald said.

"What good will that do, Vald? If you are converted, you won't be able to tell us anything," Roar said. "I have a much better idea. I let them discover me. That way, I will find out what he wants us for. At the very least, I'll find out where he put everyone."

Ruth stood up, furious. "At the very least, you could get yourself killed, Roar. Are you crazy? Anyway, how would you tell us anything if you are locked away?"

Roar smiled at her. "I'll be safe because you will come with me, and tell everyone else what you find out."

Ruth sat back down with a huff, "Stupid idea."

"But it might work," Tarek said. "Roar, are you sure?"

"I am. I'm tired of playing around the edges with this."

"Then I am coming with you," Vald said. "You get captured. I get converted. That's what that Dax will be expecting. Let's give him that. Maybe he will leave the rest of you alone. You can always wean me off his words once this is all over."

"Not necessarily," Wren muttered, but didn't try to stop the plan. It wasn't the best idea, but it gave them something to do, and she knew that Tarek was right. Something was being planned, and they needed to stop it.

It was only later that Wren asked herself how Tarek knew about Dax and Ibris, and Stryker's map. And then it was too late to matter.

Forty-Three

Meg cried herself to sleep. Since everyone was sleeping in the building with her, she couldn't let anyone hear her. Instead, Meg sobbed inside herself, and let the tears trail down her face and into the dusty cushion she was using as a pillow. Crying herself to sleep was another thing she had never experienced before.

As Meg lay there in her silent sadness, she could see why she had kept herself distant from people. This was too hard. It had been so much easier to be aloof, superior, and uncaring. Meg wondered if her mother had ever cried at night, and the thought that it was possible, and that she had caused it, made her weep even harder.

Meg knew that Ruth or Wren would ask her to pay attention to what was causing her sadness, and she realized it was so many things that it was hard to pull one out of the ball of emotions that was curled up inside of her stomach.

She was sad because she was afraid, and for what Vald had said, and because she missed her family, and because she was ordinary now at night and ashamed at herself for thinking Ordinaries were useless. It meant that at night—in her old way of thinking—she was now useless.

But what astonished her the most was that she felt sad for

others. How could that be? What difference should it make to her that other people's lives were horrid? It had never mattered before. And the realization that it mattered to her now, pulled her in so many directions she didn't know what to do. Meg felt as if the person she had been before was leaving, and someone else was taking her place.

"Ironic, isn't it?" Silke whispered, snuggling against Meg's shoulder, having silently flown across the room after sensing Meg's distress. At first, Meg turned her head away and pretended that Silke wasn't there and hadn't asked her anything. But when Silke snuggled closer, Meg gave in and asked, "What do you mean?"

"You thought being a shapeshifter was your power. And now you are shapeshifting into a different version of yourself."

"But is it a better one?" Meg whispered, trying not to sob out loud.

"It may be a harder one, but I think you will find that in the end, it is much more satisfying."

Meg sniffed and rolled over on her shoulder and wrapped her arms around Silke like she was a small doll. Not that Meg knew about snuggling dolls, but she had seen children do it. It was much more enjoyable than she thought it would be.

Meg hoped that Silke was right. That who she was becoming was going to work out in the end. But for now, it was strangely pleasant to be in a room with a group of people she was just beginning to get to know, but all of them of one mind.

This is probably what it means to have a friend, was Meg's last thought that night. As she fell asleep, she could feel Silke breathing softly, and her tiny heart beating against her chest, and felt at peace.

****

Etar's soft blue light filtered into the grimy windows of the building, illuminating Tarek sitting up against one of the walls watching over the sleepers. He smiled at the sight of Meg curled up with Silke. Silke was wide awake but hadn't moved, afraid to wake Meg. Silke winked at Tarek, and he winked back.

Vald lay snoring in the corner with his face to the wall. Wren, Ruth, and Roar were grouped together in another corner of the room. Tarek knew that the three of them had been friends for a long time, and had gone through many good and bad times together. It was going to be hard on Ruth and Wren when Roar allowed himself to be captured.

Tarek had hoped that by morning he would have come up with a better plan than Vald being converted and Roar captured. But so far, nothing better had occurred to him.

They had to find the missing Mages and get them to safety. Tarek was sure that Meg's dream was about what was going to happen to prisoners, and that meant time was running out for them.

Their plan was simple. Vald would return to the Temple and ask to be included in the conversion ceremony taking place that morning. Roar would try to stop him, and if necessary, use a little magic to make sure that the Kai-Via noticed him. Wren and Meg would follow where they took Roar, and Ruth would watch over Vald.

Tarek would contact Samis and confirm that Samis' group were not spies placed there by Dax. If all went well, Samis and his friends would be able to assist Tarek and Leon's men in freeing the Mages.

In the meantime, Silke would be following Stryker. They would eventually have to stop him too. However, it would have to be after the Mages, and their families, were safe.

It sounded easy enough. But Tarek knew that Dax would not be easily fooled. That's why they were going to have to let Vald be wholly converted, and hope that they would be able to pull him out of it when it was over. Not just Vald, but all the citizens of the Islands who had been taken in by the Preacher's words.

Something about what Ibris was doing seemed a little "off" to Tarek. Ibris' skills were tremendous. He was converting the Islands without bloodshed, assuming that the missing Mages were still alive. Tarek harbored a tiny flicker of hope that Ibris was more than a brainwashed servant of Aaron.

But there was no way to test out that premise without giving themselves away. Tarek thought that they would have to let things play out and hope that when the rebellion began, Ibris would help, or at the very least, not try to stop it.

It wouldn't be long before many of their questions would be answered. Tarek hoped that the price to find out answers to all their questions would not be too much to pay.

Forty-Four

As the conversion ceremony began, Dax settled himself into his hiding place high up in the north wall. All Temples were built basically the same, using a design that he had approved, after receiving Stryker's go-ahead.

Only the architect and the builders were aware that he had built a perch for himself inside the wall. The architect had long ago been sent to the valley of death, and after the completion of every Temple, the local builders joined him. Dax imagined that if there was a place that all living beings went to after death, there was a happy architect surrounded by people who could build him anything he could dream about.

Not that Dax believed in life after death. That was why he was going to claim all his fun here and now. There was no need to worry about a later that would never come.

Yes, Aaron-Lem promised a lovely place to go to when death's door opened, as long as they served Aaron in life. But Dax didn't believe it. After all, he had helped design those beliefs. Beliefs stolen, borrowed, and redesigned from many of the religions that used to be part of Thamon. It was genius, really. Everyone would believe in Aaron-Lem because they recognized a Truth in it that they had already accepted.

Watching the results of what he had designed was one of the reasons why Dax was hiding in the north wall. Plus, he was spying, which he enjoyed even more.

It wasn't a big space. It was just large enough for a narrow set of stairs that took him up near the ceiling of the Temple and over the heads of the Kai-Via. From his vantage point, he could see all the people gathering for the conversion ceremony. He expected to see the big man from the day before. No one knew who he was, which made it even more intriguing. Where had he come from?

Not that Dax thought that the big guy had been faking it. No, that man was ready for conversion. Who could blame him? Aaron-Lem made life so simple. Within its parameters, you would always know what to do and how to do it. Serve Aaron. Do what he asked and happiness would be yours, both in this life and in the next.

No, Dax knew that the big guy's conversion was real. What he was counting on was that his Mage friend would try and stop him. Dax thought that he might need a live Mage to help him destroy the prison camp. The Mages in the camp were too far gone to be of any help. Capturing that old Mage would be tricky, but he thought he knew exactly how he was going to do it.

Dax watched as the pool rose in the center of the Temple. That was his idea, and every time he saw it happen, it pleased him. It was beautiful. The pool was level with the floor of the Temple, making it appear as if the floor itself was water and the soon to be converted could easily step into the pool.

The water was warm and welcoming. It was even more welcoming than they knew. Yes, the Preacher's words were powerful. But drugs were too, and that was also what awaited each person as they stepped into the water.

Seeping into their bloodstream as they bowed their heads in worship was a drug that opened their minds even further to the spell of Aaron-Lem. It was also in the chalice that was sent around the Temple at every gathering. Small, micro-doses that kept their minds open to suggestions and made them feel as if they had entered heaven here and now.

No wonder the people wanted more ceremonies every day. Little did they know that what they craved was not only the drug of words but an actual drug. The head of every Kai-Via knew about the drug.

No, the head of the Kai-Via was not the Preacher as most people believed. It was a man like Dax. A man who wanted to rule and would do anything to make it happen. The Preachers were chosen for their desire to give people something good to believe in and their ability to manipulate with words and hidden suggestions.

Sometimes a Preacher discovered the drugs. Sometimes they were okay about it, and sometimes they were not. If they couldn't accept it, they were replaced. Dax didn't think Ibris had figured it out yet because knowing his old friend, Ibris would not be happy about it.

It would be hard to replace Ibris. He was the best of them all. But Stryker had made it clear that there could be no spies within the Kai-Via, and everyone found working against them would join the Mages in the prison camps or in death. Whichever came first.

Actually, death would always come, which brought Dax back to the present. It was time to find the person that would help him with his current problem: destroying the prison camp.

The low hum began, and the Kai-Via entered. That hum was another drug. A sound drug. Not everyone was impacted by it, but many were. As the hum swelled, Ibris walked in, and the silence gathered and became a presence filling every space within the temple walls.

Standing with the Kai-Via, Dax sucked in his breath. There he was. He was hard to miss. Standing in the middle of the crowd was the big man from yesterday's gathering. Yes, he was a goner. His face registered nothing but pure bliss.

The ravens weren't there. Dax wasn't surprised. Those two shapeshifters would be idiots to show up looking the same way each time. But Dax was sure that they were around somewhere. He was going to have to be very smart in capturing that Mage because Dax was sure it was all part of a plan. One that he was going to turn to his advantage.

Forty-Five

Every pore of Ruth's being was focused on Roar as he kept his attention on Vald. Wren and Meg were responsible for Vald. She was responsible for Roar.

Not just because he had chosen to be a complete idiot and let himself be captured, but because he was her friend. They had been friends long before that tyrant, Aaron, and the big-headed, small-minded freak, Stryker, got together and decided that to take over the world all they had to do was start a religion, and then sell it to the masses.

Sell it, force it. It was all the same. Ruth suspected that there was more than just the power of words, and the conscious and subconscious suggestions that the Preachers had mastered. But she hadn't been able to prove it yet.

Right now, that wasn't her main problem. The problem she was having was keeping an eye on that crazy Mage, Roar. There was nothing she could have done to stop him, and he was counting on her not to lose him after his capture.

The plan sounded simple enough, but the crowd at the Temple was massive and growing bigger every moment. People were standing shoulder to shoulder, and it was getting harder and harder for her to follow Roar as he made his way through the press of people. At first, she shifted to look like an older woman in the crowd. But pushing through people to stay close to Roar proved too difficult, so she shifted into a mouse and scampered after Roar's legs as he followed Vald.

Vald was easy to follow. He stuck out above the crowd, and Ruth almost wished her assignment was to follow him. However, she knew she would not be happy with that assignment. Roar was hers to protect.

Their mothers had been best friends, which threw the two of them together all the time as children. Their mothers would meet at the market for a quick coffee, or visit each other's homes, taking their children along with them. Roar and Ruth were the only shapeshifters in their family who were not tied to just one type of transformation. Which meant they were hard to control.

One day, Ruth almost died while they were playing a game of how many different people, or beings, they could be in a five-minute time span. Roar revived her and the two of them had learned their lesson. Together they had decided to only shapeshift for a good reason, and never to harm or annoy people using their abilities.

It had been hard at first to break the habit, but watching both their mothers relax for the first time in years as their shapeshifter children tamed themselves, made it worthwhile.

Many people believed that Ruth and Roar would marry when they grew up, but they knew they wouldn't. They had a different kind of relationship.

Roar had no desire to marry and was thrilled when Ruth married and had children. Now her family was in hiding, and Roar was trying to be a hero.

Not for the first time, Ruth shook her head in frustration with Roar's decision. No, he wasn't breaking their agreement.

He was doing this for a good reason, but it was making every one of her nerves stand on end.

****

Meg and Wren watched from the edge of the crowd. Meg thought she made a fine-looking young man, holding his daughter's hand. Except the daughter had insisted on riding on Meg's shoulders.

"You're too heavy," Meg had hissed at Wren, who only pulled her hair in return.

"Do you see him?" Wren whispered in Meg's ear.

Meg, who had never had someone riding on her shoulders before, was trying to adjust to standing under Wren's weight, when she spotted Vald making his way towards the pool.

"I see Vald, but which one of the Kai-Via is Dax? Maybe he isn't here, and this is a waste of time."

"He's here," Wren whispered back. "He knows something is going on, so he'll be watching today."

Meg hissed under her breath, "Watching so he can capture us, you mean."

Wren didn't bother to answer. She didn't want to be riding on Meg's shoulders any more than Meg wanted her to, but they had a job to do: stay with Vald.

After every ceremony, the newly converted were whisked off somewhere and then returned a few hours later. No one ever spoke about what happened there. Maybe they didn't remember? But if they could follow Vald, they would find out for themselves, and perhaps that would give them a clue to what Dax was planning.

Only Wren would be able to continue to stay with Vald. Meg would have to return to the old building every night. At least it wouldn't be empty. Tarek would be there, and Silke too, of course.

But if Meg was truthful with herself, which she was trying to be, she couldn't wait to see Tarek again.

He scared her. Everything about him frightened her. The things he said. The way he looked. What he expected of her. But still. She couldn't wait to see him again. And she was going to make him proud of her if it killed her doing it.

Wren snorted in her ear. "Seriously? Don't worry about making him proud—just do your job."

Meg was tempted to throw Wren off her shoulders, but that would give them away. After all, what father would throw their daughter off their shoulders? But she needed to remember that all of her new "friends" could also read her thoughts. At least some of them.

"Look," Wren said.

Meg could see Vald stepping into the pool, his face radiating pure happiness. A part of Meg wished for him that he could stay there, in that feeling. Was it so wrong to be that happy?

As they watched, a commotion began as Roar screamed, "No!" and began pushing through the crowd. Meg wondered where Ruth was, but knew that she was somewhere close. She would never let Roar out of her sight. Everything was going as planned.

But then something happened that no one expected. Instead of the usual lovely twinkling mist dropping from the ceiling, a fog descended, wrapping everyone in a deep gray cocoon.

"I can't see anything," Wren said, and then just as quickly as it had come, the fog lifted as if it had never been there in the first place.

"Where are they?" Meg asked, spinning around looking for Vald and Roar.

"We've lost them," Wren said.

The two of them stared at the crowd, who seemed unperturbed by what had happened. As if the worst scenario hadn't just taken place before their eyes.

"Maybe Ruth has them," Meg said.

"I don't," Ruth answered, standing beside them looking as if she had lost her best friend, which of course was exactly what had happened.

Roar and Vald were gone, and they had no idea where they were.

Forty-Six

Tarek shook his head, trying to make sense of what the three women were trying to tell him. But the fact that they were in front of him, instead of following Roar and Vald, told him all he needed to know. They had lost them.

They were meeting in the deserted building just as they had planned, but not for this early in the day. Wren had stopped in at the market, found Tarek, and told him there was a problem. He had flicked a wrist, and a split second later they were in the building. In spite of her terror at losing Vald and Roar, Wren couldn't help wishing that she too had that ability.

"What are we going to do?" Ruth begged Tarek, hoping that he would have an answer. She couldn't believe that she had let her best friend down. She was terrified that Roar was being tortured at this very moment, and it was her fault.

"We are going to wait until Silke and Samis return," Tarek answered. "They are our backup plan, and since neither one of them is here, I am assuming that they didn't lose Roar or Vald."

All three women sat down on the floor of the building at the same time as if all the air had gone out of them.

"Why didn't you tell us?" Meg demanded, not sure if she should be happy about it or angry because she hadn't known.

"We didn't tell you so that you wouldn't give them away," Tarek said, sitting on the floor in front of them.

"After you told us yesterday that Dax knew that you were there, we knew that it was possible he would have a plan in place to capture all of you. The fact that he didn't find the three of you means that he wasn't able to figure out who you are. Good job, by the way," Tarek added, making sure he addressed Meg as he said it, knowing how much she would appreciate the validation.

"But, of course, since we made sure that he knew about Vald and Roar, he was able to capture them as we planned. However, we assumed that he would have a trick up his sleeve, so Silke hid inside Roar's coat, and Samis was right beside Vald."

"I didn't see Samis beside Vald," Meg said.

"No, you didn't. I put a block in all your minds so you couldn't. So you wouldn't give Samis away by mistake. So when Vald converted, Samis was right there with him."

"But Samis is Ordinary, isn't he? Won't he be converted too?"

It was Wren who understood right away. "Samis is immune to it somehow, isn't he?"

"He is, and so is the small group he has gathered for us. Samis has wanted to infiltrate the conversion ceremony for a while, so it was the perfect opportunity for him. He and Silke will come here after they get the information we need. In the meantime, get some rest. Once they return, we will have to move quickly."

As much as they wanted to rest, no one could. Tarek had vanished, saying that he would be back, and that made it worse because they knew they were being left out of the plans. The three women tried small talk, but eventually gave up. Each one of them sat alone, thinking about what they could have done better.

Meg was so restless that Wren finally asked her to go to another corner to wait. Then seeing Meg's crestfallen face, she apologized and patted the dusty pillow beside her.

"It's just that now it is almost night, and I will be helpless again," Meg said. "You'll all go off to rescue Roar, Vald, and the Mages, and I'll be sitting here waiting, not being of any use at all."

Wren knew that she should be giving Meg some kind of encouragement. Explain that the lack of magical skill did not make her useless. But the words stuck in her throat because at that moment she felt just as useless, and the fact that neither Silke, Tarek, or Samis had returned made everything seem so much worse.

It was almost morning before the three of them materialized in the middle of the room, startling the half-asleep women who were hoping against hope for a miracle.

Meg surprised herself and everyone else when she stumbled over to Silke with tears in her eyes, and almost crushed her against her chest. Silke, looking bedraggled and exhausted managed to not squeal in protest, but allowed Meg to hug her for a moment before flying back to Tarek's shoulder.

Samis stood in place with his mouth open, holding a bag, trying to process what had just happened. He had never been transported somewhere before and found it both pleasant and disturbing.

Not knowing what else to do, he held out the bag and stuttered, "Food?"

No one moved until Tarek took an orange out of the bag, nodded at Samis, and sat down in the exact spot he had been at the beginning of the night. After everyone had taken food, Tarek said, "Well, we know where Roar is, and we have an idea what Dax is planning. But we are going to need more help."

Ruth held onto the apple that she had taken as if it was a lifeline, afraid to ask the obvious question. Where were they going to get more help, and was Roar alright? And why didn't they bring Vald back with them?

Tarek looked at Ruth, and a wave of sadness passed over him. "Vald wouldn't come back with us. He wanted to stay with the converted, and we couldn't get to Roar. Dax is using him to destroy the camp and us if we interfere."

Forty-Seven

The old man, the one Dax knew was a Mage, and his big friend were lying stretched out on a rough plank of Stonenut wood. Their arms were extended over their heads, locked inside metal bands bolted to the wood. Their legs were spread apart, each one attached to a short chain also bolted to the plank.

If they struggled, they would have a momentary feeling that perhaps they could move and kick the chains off, but instead what it would do would stretch out the table, pulling their bodies apart. Dax smiled to himself, happy with his handiwork. The room they were in was another unique feature of all of the Temples. It existed underneath the main floor, on the same level as the pool when it was not in use.

He could see the pool water glowing in the blue light that he had installed to light the area. The water looked so innocent, nothing marring its surface. No one knew how dangerous that pool water was, or how many people had died in it, held down by his hand when they didn't give him what he wanted, or just for the pleasure of it. Dax loved how water never gave its secrets away. Like him.

Usually, the door to his secret room was closed, and invisible to everyone. No one in all of Thamon knew that his hidden place existed. Even if they did, they would never be able to enter it. The doors opened only for him. But when there was no one else at the Temple, Dax loved to open the doors and enjoy the view of the pool and his handwork.

The pool was shallow so that even the shortest Islander could stand during the conversion ceremony, and that made it easy for him to pour the drugs into the water before the entire pool rose to the surface for the conversion ceremony. The drugging of the pool was not a secret. Every head of the Kai-Via knew how to put the drugs into the pool and the chalices.

To keep anyone from suspecting, and to avoid deaths of Aaron-Lem followers, no one was ever allowed in the pool except during conversion ceremonies. Stryker and Aaron did not want any undue attention brought to the pool.

Dax loved the pool, and called it the Killing Pool but only to himself. Yes, every member of the Kai-Via and the Preacher knew about the location of the pool, but only he knew of the room built into every Temple beside the pool. And since no one was allowed below the floor of the Temple without the head of the Kai-Via, there was never a chance of anyone discovering it.

Leaning against the door frame, Dax cleaned his nails with his knife. He always had it with him. It was a gift given to every head of the Kai-Via by Stryker.

The knives were all the same, except their names were engraved on the handles. It was a special knife. It sat safely in the pocket of his robe, but with a touch of a button, it sprang to life, useful within a split second. Dax couldn't begin to count the times his little knife had enabled the capture or the death of an enemy of Aaron-Lem.

Holding the knife soothed him. Using it thrilled him. Finished with his nails, Dax looked into the room where his two prisoners were resting.

The Mage was motionless. Dax had injected him with a unique drug that paralyzed him but kept him alert enough to answer questions. It was what Dax had used on all the Mages. Otherwise, there was no way to keep them after capturing them. It kept part of them awake, the part that could understand what was happening to them and those around them, but couldn't do anything about it. Dax figured it felt like a living hell, just what he needed them to feel.

The big one was wide awake. The drug from the pool and the extra drink he had received after the ceremony, had worn off a while ago. But he had not reacted when he found himself bound to the stretching table.

Instead, he stared at the ceiling and smiled. It was creeping Dax out. It was not the response he needed or wanted. He had managed to get his name, Vald. But not where he had come from. He wasn't one of the Islanders, that was evident. Probably someone who had deserted his ship.

It didn't matter. The big guy was only of use to Dax as a tool to get the old Mage to help him destroy the prison camp. On the other hand, perhaps Vald would give up who the three shapeshifters were who had been at the Temple.

Dax threw the knife at the pool's wall in irritation. He had fully expected to capture all of them. But even though he was watching for them, he never saw anything that gave away their location. He could only feel their presence, but not track it to any particular person, or bird. He figured that they were probably birds because it was so easy to fly away.

Oh, well, Dax thought. *It gives me a good reason for having a little fun before the big event.* Dax retrieved the knife from the wall, making a note to have the hole repaired, and headed towards the bare feet of the big guy who was still staring and smiling at the ceiling. He wouldn't be smiling much longer.

When Dax turned away for a second, a small spider dropped from the ceiling to Vald's neck, bit him, and quickly returned to the ceiling.

Vald continued to smile, even as he felt the first prick of the knife.

Forty-Eight

Aaron was infuriated. How could this be happening? He was still shaking from anger at what he had learned. At first, his spies had been afraid to tell him what they had found. For a good reason, it turned out, because after they told him all that he needed to know, they were all incinerated with one blast from his hand. He had not used magic. He had used technology. What was the difference?

Aaron had instructed the most brilliant of his followers to design a way for him to shoot laser beams any time that he wanted to—at anyone or anything. It had taken longer than Aaron had wanted, but eventually, they had designed him an almost invisible contraption he wore around his wrist.

When activated, it looked like a beam of light shooting out from the palm of his hands. Those designers were his first trial subjects. It worked, and now those designers were gone, no one left to give his secret away.

Aaron had other designers working on more ideas. They were also expendable. What wasn't expendable was the power he held over the people because he was their God.

Magic or technology, who cared which one he used? All he was looking for was results, and the wrist band always produced results. He had the engineers make him extras in case one failed. Aaron always prepared for the worst. Why not? Aaron knew things always went wrong. How could they not? Besides, he was often the cause of the worst happening.

The fact that he didn't have any natural magic, and had always felt inferior to those that had, was part of the reason Aaron banned magic. It didn't help that the non-magical were called Ordinaries.

He was definitely not ordinary, and he had decided early on in life to make sure no one ever called him that. When he blasted fire from his hands, or blinded, or levitated with the use of tricks, he told his followers it was not magic but the power of the one true God seen by them, mere mortals.

Magic ran a poor second to being a god. Especially when he was eliminating all the Mages from Thamon. That left him as God and everyone else as Ordinary. What could be better than that? Except when things went wrong.

And now it appeared as if one of the scenarios that he thought would never happen, was in process. Of course, it was possible that Stryker was doing it all for him, and wanted it to be a surprise. He and Stryker had been friends for so long that Aaron didn't want to believe that Stryker would move against him.

After his anger had faded, that's what Aaron decided was happening. Stryker was preparing a surprise for him. He would let Stryker have time to do whatever he was doing on the Islands. His spies had mentioned that Stryker had a map that he looked at every day. It must be a map for a treasure. And even if Stryker wasn't getting it for him, he would have it sooner or later.

Sighing, Aaron realized that he would have to send out more spies. First, he'd have to find some, now that those three were gone. Aaron looked at the pile of ashes lying on the floor and ordered the servant standing in the corner to have it cleaned immediately. Aaron could see the servant was trembling from head to toe, trying to control his fear so that Aaron wouldn't notice. At first, Aaron thought of punishing him for showing fear, but changed his mind. After all, he had no idea what had happened.

Oh, wait, Aaron thought. *He does know what happened.* He heard what they said. Now, Aaron understood why the servant was trembling. Probably best to put him out of his misery. *Who says I don't have compassion,* Aaron thought as he used his laser again.

Flicking his black robes to the side, Aaron rose. There was no one left in the room with him. He'd have to find more Blessed Ones to clean up the mess.

Aaron was undecided about Stryker. He needed a sign to tell him what to do. A walk in the garden should do the trick. After instructing one of the Blessed Ones to do what he wanted, Aaron walked out into his gardens, tended by more blind servants.

It was amazing what they could do without sight. They could hear him coming and bowed as he passed. Although he wanted to be alone to think, Aaron couldn't help but feel pleasure having so many people look up to him.

Should he go to the Islands to see what Stryker was up to, or wait to find out what Stryker was doing? The idea of traveling on a ship didn't appeal to him at all. A flash of blue light happened as Etar and Trin crossed each other. *A sign, He was needed here.* The Kai-Via need new rituals to spice up the ceremonies.

Aaron was clear. It would be better to spend his time on rituals and training someone to take Stryker's place in case

Stryker turned out to be a traitor.

Besides, his palace was a paradise. It had everything he needed to be happy. Why leave it when there was work that he could do in his private heaven?

A ship, no matter how well-appointed and staffed, would always be less comfortable than home. The fact that it would also be more dangerous also came into play. It was harder to control his environment out on the seas. No, he would stay home and train replacements for anyone who had decided to have more power than him, even if it was his friend, Stryker.

Aaron had someone in mind. The man he had in mind had also been a member of their class in school. But until now, Aaron had kept him in the background.

Even Stryker didn't know that Aaron had built an alliance with him. However, he needed more training, and although they were friends, he would still have to test him.

Now that sounds like fun, Aaron thought, as he headed out of the room to summon servants, find new spies, and check on Stryker's replacement.

You can never be too careful, Aaron thought. But first maybe a visit to the women of the Blessed Ones. He had worked hard this morning. It was time for some relief.

Forty-Nine

Dax had what he wanted. The machine that Stryker had given each head of the Kai-Via worked like a charm. Aaron had forbidden its use except for emergencies, but Dax had used it anyway on the Mage that he now knew was called Roar.

And even though Dax hadn't been sure before, now he knew it was a real emergency. But he was not going to share the information with Stryker, because Stryker might try to take his response to what he had learned away from him, and Dax wanted the pleasure to be all his.

I might have been wrong about the big guy, though, Dax thought. Perhaps he was an innocent bystander who really was one of the converted. After a period of torture it turned out that the big guy didn't know anything. It had been a waste of energy to try and get anything out of him. Disposing of him would have to wait. Now that he was dead, Dax couldn't use him as a leverage point for making the Mage work faster. That was a pity. But he probably didn't need him after all.

The machine was a marvel. It sucked all the thoughts out of a person. Even Mages couldn't resist it, and although Roar had held out longer than most, eventually he had told Dax all that he knew.

The Mage had confirmed what Dax had believed. Yes, there was an organized rebellion on the Islands. However, it was much bigger than he had thought.

When Dax had banished all the Mages to the prison camp, he had never intended to let them live, but the torturing had been so much fun he hadn't wanted it to end. Except he had agreed to follow Stryker's orders and destroy the camp. Now he needed to do it as quickly as possible. The Mage had told him that there was a plan in place to rescue the prisoners.

Actually, that was good news. The rebels would all be at the camp, trying to rescue the Mages. Instead, they would become part of the destruction of the prison. He could trap them all and end it with one big event.

Those three shapeshifters that he had felt in the Temple would be there too. One of them was new to the Islands, along with a new wizard.

Dax was tempted to try and capture the wizard and the new shapeshifter to find out where they had come from, but it would be too dangerous, and at the moment he didn't have time for danger. Stryker was on the Islands for a reason, and he needed to find out why. No, he would let the Mage help destroy them all, leaving the field clear for him to deal with Stryker. And Ibris. There was always Ibris. He knew something was going on with him, too.

No, Dax didn't have time to let the rebellion drag out. He had enough to deal with without Mages and rebels giving him trouble.

Glancing back into the room, Dax folded his knife and put it into his robe. As a member of the Kai-Via, no one would dare question him as he took care of business.

Dax was grateful that the Mage didn't look too heavy. Releasing Roar from the restraints, Dax hoisted him up and helped him stand by letting him put all his weight on him. *This was not going to be fun, having a Mage up so close,* he thought.

Dax dragged Roar from the room, closing the secret door behind him, catching one last glimpse of the dead man on the table. He wasn't going anywhere.

Silke waited until Dax had taken Roar from the room, and closed the door before dropping once again to the table where Vald lay. Another bite on his neck and he started breathing again. Still smiling.

******

Back in the deserted building, Silke did her best to share what had happened, but she was exhausted. Samis stood next to her looking just as tired.

"Yes," she said to the astonished gathering, "I can shapeshift if necessary, but I have only done it a few times in my life. I don't like it. At all."

She leaned against Tarek's cheek and whispered something. Tarek smiled and said, "Yes, I'll take Samis to Vald. He'll be fine."

"Okay," Tarek said to the group. "We can't let Roar down. He did what he needed to do, but that leaves us a small window of time to run the rescue. Is everyone ready?"

Meg had her arm around Ruth and asked the question that Ruth couldn't. "Will Roar be alright?"

"I don't know," Tarek said, "But if we want to honor him, we have to succeed. It's what he would want. Ruth, we are going to need you to be fully present. Can you do it?"

Meg answered for Ruth. "Yes, she can. We can," she said, reaching for Ruth's and Wren's hands.

Tarek looked at the three women and smiled. "Alright, you

know what you have to do. Dax knows who you are now, and he thinks that gives him the advantage. Prove him wrong."

With that, he, Silke, and Samis vanished.

Meg turned to Ruth and Wren and asked, "Shall we?"

Turning into ravens, the three of them flew from the room. After all, Dax would be looking for ravens. Might as well give him what he was expecting.

Fifty

The trip to the prison camp took much longer than Dax had expected. The Mage was barely functioning, and Dax had to keep finding ways to keep him from falling asleep, or tipping out of the cart. Dax suspected that Roar was faking it so that he wouldn't be asked to help destroy the prison camp. Dax snickered to himself. It didn't matter. Yes, he needed the Mage, but not the way Roar thought. He could destroy the camp without his help.

Roar was bait, that's all he was. Dax wanted Roar's friends to come for him, so they would be present when the earthquake began, dropping the camp and all its inhabitants down into the earth, disappearing them forever. If all went as planned, the quake would open a passageway to the lake on the other side of the camp. Water would rush in and flood the area.

Even if that didn't happen, the earthquake would be enough. Now that Dax had the names of all the people working against him, he would be sure that they were present when the quake struck. He would be killing all those rebels and Mages with just one stroke.

He had been planning on how to trigger an earthquake for a long time. Long before Stryker asked him to destroy the camp, Dax had a plan in the works. He knew someday it would become necessary to eliminate all the evidence of what he had done. What made the idea so brilliant was he was using the Mages to cause their own destruction. To earn the meager amount of food they received every day, they had to work for it. Giant drills driven by the labor of the prisoners had been working for months digging down into the Island's core.

What came next was a result of something Dax had stolen from Aaron years before. Long ago, when he and Ibris were still apprentices, they had accompanied Stryker on a trip to Aaron's palace. Both of them were still at the stage of infatuation with everything that Stryker had taught them, and to visit Aaron was both terrifying and exhilarating.

While they were there, Aaron had punished one of his servants with fire from his hands, turning the servant into a pile of ash. Dax was spellbound, and Ibris was horrified. Later Stryker had explained to them both that Aaron had the right to take life and the power to do it because he was God.

Dax doubted that the explanation appeased Ibris, but he knew it didn't satisfy him. He wanted to know how Aaron did it. Magic was banned. So it couldn't be magic. What was it that Aaron had used? Dax was determined to find out. That night he followed Aaron and saw him take something off his wrist and place it in a chest which he then locked.

Later, Dax's curiosity overrode his fear of being discovered, and he snuck into Aaron's room after everyone was asleep. Using a skill his father had taught him before he died, Dax picked the lock and found the chest filled with wrist bands. He didn't hesitate. He took one. There were so many Dax knew that Aaron wouldn't know if one was missing, and even if he did, he would never suspect Dax.

It was months before Dax was able to sneak off into the

woods to figure out what it was. He almost killed himself when he held the band instead of putting it on and somehow triggered it. A laser beam had shot out, missing him by a few inches and hitting a tree behind him. The tree disintegrated, and so did the one behind it. All that was left was a pile of ash.

Dax had discovered Aaron's secret. Aaron was just a man who knew how to wield power. Perhaps that made him a god, Dax didn't care. As long as he got what he wanted, Aaron could do whatever he wanted to do, too. It was much later before Dax figured out that Aaron and Stryker were behind the destruction of his village. But by then, Dax was already on his path to power, and he added revenge into his plans.

For years, Dax kept the powerful band hidden. He told no one that he had it. He never let on that he didn't believe in Aaron's power or Stryker's right to rule over him. It didn't matter what they thought. He knew what he was doing.

Dax had tested the wrist band only a few times after that to make sure it worked, but always cautiously when there was no chance that anyone would see him. He was waiting for the perfect time to use it. A time when no one would suspect that it had been used.

Now was the time. An earthquake, the destruction of the empire, and he would be the ruler. In time he would use it against Stryker and Aaron. But he wasn't in any rush. He wasn't in any rush. He would let Aaron and Stryker fight it out, let them be the face of Aaron-Lem, but behind the scenes he would be running things, just the way he was now.

******

Roar allowed himself to be shoved into the cart. He let his weight drop onto Dax, making Dax push him aside over and over again. Roar figured that Dax would hate being touched by a Mage, so it gave Roar pleasure doing even this small thing to irritate him. Roar was taking all the pleasure he could because otherwise he might be focused too much on the fear that gripped him.

In spite of all the planning that he and Tarek had done, Roar was still worried. The machine was much harder to control then any of them had considered. Without Silke's help, he would have succumbed to the pain and said anything, but instead, he said only what he wanted Dax to hear.

Still, Roar was worried that he might have said more than he meant to while he was drugged and attached to that soul-sucking machine.

Silke was the hero. She had shifted herself into a spider hidden inside his jacket. Silke had countered the drug Dax gave him and given him a pain stopping drug as soon as they entered the room.

Roar knew that once this was over, he was going to have to find a way to thank Silke for putting her life at risk to keep him and Vald safe. Not that Vald had been entirely safe. Dax had fun with the knife. Even though Roar knew that Vald was still alive, protected by Silke, his recovery might take a long time.

Roar knew what was going to happen once they reached the camp. Dax had been so sure of himself he told Roar, thinking that he would soon be dead anyway.

Dax was going to destroy the prison camp with an earthquake.

But first, he would wait for Roar's friends to come to rescue him and get them all with one fell swoop. It was brilliant, really. Everyone would think it was a natural disaster, and there would be no evidence proving otherwise.

Roar knew that his friends were on the way. The timing was

critical. Would they be able to rescue the prisoners before the quake, or would they all be caught in the destruction that Dax had planned?

All he could do was continue to irritate Dax and try to stop him from doing whatever he was going to do to trigger the earthquake, until everyone was safe, and hope that was enough.

Fifty-One

Not far from the prison camp, Stryker stood in a clearing looking at the map one more time. After all this time and effort, he wasn't sure if he had come to the right place after all.

What if the map was fake? What if everything he had learned about the pendant wasn't real? What if he had based his life on a lie? Stryker had asked these same questions of himself many times before. But this time he was so close to where he thought the treasure would be, that Stryker was afraid that he had been wrong all along.

What if all that he had heard about the treasure was only a myth? What if he had wasted his life on nothing but empty stories? Yes, he had found many writings that spoke of the gold pendant with the ruby in the middle that gave its wearer the power to control others.

The man who had worn it before had been considered a god. But one day, it had been stolen. And instead of wearing it and claiming its power, the thief had hidden it where no one could find it.

Why a map then? Stryker had asked himself that question over and over again. The answer he had always come up with was that the thief had hidden the pendant until the right person could find it. And since he had the map, he must be the right person.

There is no reason not to believe that now, he told himself. Yes, he had felt discouraged before, but he always pulled himself out of the slump. He had to believe in what he was doing more than ever before. It had to be true. He would find the treasure that would change not only his life, but the life, of every person in Thamon.

Every time Stryker unfolded the map, it was different. Sometimes it showed him pictures. Sometimes words, and not always the same ones. He never knew what the map would reveal. Yes, he knew that meant that the map was magical. It was one reason Stryker went along with Aaron's plan to banish all magic. There could never be another map like this. If they were still alive, the Mage or Mages that made it would be killed along with every other Mage on Thamon. He alone would have the secret to ultimate power.

Today there were no words on the map, just a picture. Yes, it was definitely the Islands. There were two landmasses with a land bridge between them. There was no place else on Thamon that looked just like this other than these Islands. Stryker sighed, happy that the map had confirmed for him what he needed to be assured of again. He was in the right place. And now that it had been confirmed, Stryker was sure that he was right about where he would find the pendant. Soon he would be the ruler of Thamon.

He would be able to project any thought he wanted to into anyone's mind. Ordinaries and Mages alike. It wouldn't matter. Once the treasure was his no one would ever be able to stand against him. He would not only be able to read all thought, but he would also be able to direct everyone to do his bidding.

It was ironic that it wasn't the map that had shown him the

exact spot where to find the pendant. It was the storm that had forced him and Dax into the cave.

Was it fate that sent them there? It didn't matter. He had received the final clue while waiting for the storm to end. A rough drawing of a man wearing the pendant was illuminated when lightning had flashed through the cave. At the time, he had gasped, and Dax thought it was the lightning that shocked him. Instead, it was the fulfillment of a lifelong dream, and he couldn't tell anyone. Especially Dax.

But it was the real reason he had told Dax to hold off on destroying the prison camp. He had needed the extra time to make sure everything was in place for him to leave the Islands once he secured the pendant.

If Dax followed what he had asked him to do, tomorrow was the day that Dax would destroy the camp, but he would be long gone, pendant safe in his keeping.

Folding the map and putting it back in his pocket, Stryker headed to the cave. After seeing the picture on the wall in the cave, he had secretly marked the trees as he and Dax had made their way back to the Temple so it would be easy to find again.

A shadow passed over Trin, and Stryker glanced up just in time to see three ravens heading towards the prison camp. But he thought nothing of it. He was focused on the pendant and the end of his long search for power.

****

Ibris lowered himself to his knees and bowed so that his forehead rested on the floor of his room. He wished that he could stay there forever, letting the breeze wash over him, momentarily releasing him from his self-imposed prison.

Ibris knew if someone could see him, they would think that

he was bowing to Aaron, as required of any convert to Aaron-Lem.

Only Ibris knew that he was not bowing to Aaron. He was bowing to the God that he believed in, hoping that he would hear a direct answer to his question.

But he knew the answer already, and he didn't like it. And yet he knew it was what he would have to do. Could he do it without revealing himself? If he could only figure out how to rescue Stryker without him knowing how it happened, they would both be safe.

Stryker would be safe from the destruction that Dax was planning, and he would be safe from anyone knowing his secret. He'd have to come up with a solution soon. There wasn't much time left.

Fifty-Two

Tarek's first stop was the Market. Although Samis was busy rescuing Vald, the small group of men and women that Samis had gathered were waiting at his booth, ready to do whatever they needed to do. Even after Tarek explained the danger, they didn't hesitate. They couldn't sit by any longer watching their neighbors and friends disappear, or become slaves to Aaron.

Instead of leaving the Market quietly, Tarek told the group to make sure that people noticed them as they walked the Arrow to Hetale. It worked. People turned to look at them, and that was what they wanted. Tarek had reminded them that members of the Kai-Via would be watching. Without their black robes on no one would know who they were, but they were there, always spying to make sure that everyone was behaving correctly as a member of Aaron-Lem.

The Kai-Via would wonder where the group was going, especially if they kept on walking when they should be on their knees praying to Aaron.

The group was to keep moving in the direction of the prison camp. Some, maybe all of the Kai-Via, would follow. But since Dax wouldn't be there, they would not do anything. At least that was what Tarek hoped.

The goal was to be a distraction, but without getting arrested. Fight if they needed to, but keep moving. However, they were not to go into the camp under any circumstances.

Once Samis' group was on their way, Tarek transported himself to outside the camp where Meg, Wren, and Ruth were waiting for him.

"Are you ready?" Tarek asked.

The three of them nodded. Tarek waited. He knew there was more. All three women could barely look at him.

"What's going on?" he asked.

It was Meg who answered. "We don't understand how this could be happening. It's one thing to hear that Mages have disappeared and that there are prison camps, but it's entirely different seeing it. The people that are still alive are locked in cages. How could anyone do this?"

"People look the other way thinking it doesn't affect them, Meg," Tarek answered. "Or they start believing that some people are less than them. Aaron and Stryker learned how to suggest things to people in ways that fulfilled desires or alleviated fears. They discovered that telling lies wrapped in a truth works when they can get people to stop thinking and walk away from compassion and understanding.

"As long as people believe that there is not enough for everyone, people will suffer. In Stryker and Aaron's case, it's power that they want, and no matter how much of it they have, it will never be enough.

"Aaron and Stryker believe that if they eliminate everyone who can think clearly in spite of the lies they tell, then they will be free to do whatever they want to do. They find pleasure in ruling over others."

"How can it give them pleasure to put people in cages and treat them like animals?" Meg cried.

"It's part of winning the game that they have constructed. Aaron and Stryker have convinced themselves that the world would be better without thinkers and Mages, so they are banishing them for what they believe is all the right reasons.

"For Stryker, Aaron, and the Kai-Via leaders like Dax, they believe that they are the wise ones who know best, and caging, mistreating, and killing those that oppose them is their right."

"Which we are going to take away from them," Silke said, materializing on Tarek's shoulder.

Seeing Meg's distress, Silke added, "This is not the time to be discouraged. If you want to hole up somewhere after this is over and mourn what has happened, I might join you. But right now we need to save those people, and it will take all of us to do it.

"I made a few stops to check on arrival times. Two Kai-Via are following Samis' group. One Kai-Via has run ahead, looking for Dax. I'll make sure he finds him. Dax will have to stop and decide what to do about them, which should stall him even more. Roar has done a great job of slowing him down."

Hearing Ruth gasp, Silke flew to her and kissed her on the cheek. "He's doing okay. Still weak, but that's working in his favor since Dax thinks that Roar is disabled. He's not. He'll be ready to help when we need it."

Silke continued, while everyone pretended not to notice the tear that broke free and ran down Ruth's cheek. "As you predicted, Tarek, Stryker is on his own, heading towards the cave. He keeps pulling out that map and muttering to himself. I think he is afraid that he is in the wrong place."

"Or that he is in the right one," Tarek said.

Silke nodded. "True. Either way, he is moving slowly, but he might make it to the cave, and if he does, I am not sure if he'll be safe there. Do you want me to stop him?"

"What do you mean?" Meg shouted. "Don't you want him

to die? He's evil. He's doing evil."

Tarek leveled his gaze at Meg and said, "But we aren't."

Meg turned away, feeling confused and ashamed at the same time.

"Not now," Wren hissed at Meg. "Feel bad later. We need you now."

"How many guards?" Tarek asked, and Ruth answered. "Four that we could see. There isn't much to guard. Everyone alive is locked in a cage."

"Okay. You all know the plan. We have to let Dax think that all the people in the camp are destroyed. The three of you will help Roar create the illusion that the prisoners are still there. As shapeshifters, you can be the people he expects to see, while Roar makes it appear that there are more of you.

"Silke and I are going to transport people out a few at a time, starting with the guards so that we won't have anyone stopping us from releasing everyone."

"You are taking the guards to the cave, too?" Meg asked, trying to show that she had gotten over herself.

It was something she was getting better at, but was realizing more and more how self-centered she had been. She wanted to prove to herself that perhaps she could do more than Tarek expected and he would be proud of her.

However, even without hearing Silke's or Wren's voice in her head, she knew that she had to be proud of herself first. She would keep watching for an opportunity to do more. She didn't doubt that it would occur.

Tarek nodded and disappeared along with Silke.

"Are you ready?" Wren asked.

Ruth and Meg tilted their heads and then transformed into ravens.

Before heading to the camp, they needed to fly over Dax

and Roar. They hoped to disturb Dax and slow him down as he questioned what they were doing there.

But mostly they wanted to assure Roar that the plan was in process.

Fifty-Three

Dax saw the three ravens and snickered to himself. He knew who they were, and he knew that they wanted him to know. They wanted him to be worried. Of course, they were up to something, but so was he!

He wanted those shapeshifters to be at the camp, trying to save the prisoners when he released the earthquake. Getting rid of four shapeshifters at one time would earn him points with Aaron and Stryker. That might come in handy in the future.

A few minutes before the ravens had flown over, the Kai-Via runner had caught up with him and told him about the group that was heading towards the camp. Dax knew about the rebel leader of that group, too. Roar had told him during his session with the machine.

Dax hoped that the man Samis would be part of the group following him. Perhaps these were all Ordinaries, but the power of the Preacher's words didn't affect them. That made them dangerous. And besides, Samis had fooled him, and that would never do.

It amazed Dax that all of these people could think he would be so stupid not to know what they were doing. Of course, they were trying to slow him down so they could rescue the prisoners first. Glancing over at the man hanging off the cart, he smiled. He even knew what Roar was doing. He was trying to distract him, trying to make him think that he was too weak to do anything.

What Dax didn't understand was why Roar wasn't weak. Something had happened in that room that he hadn't seen. He would love to interrogate Roar again, but there probably wasn't time. It didn't matter. Roar would be dead soon like the rest of them.

Dax had instructed the runner to start pushing the group that was following him faster towards the camp. He wanted the group to be close enough to be part of the destruction, too. Just thinking about the damage he was planning made Dax flush with pleasure.

He would be accomplishing so many things at once. Stryker would be pleased. Yes, he had pushed the camp destruction up by a day, and Stryker didn't know that.

But Dax didn't think that it would make much difference to Stryker. He would be happy that Dax had destroyed the camp the way he had wanted. It would look like a natural event. All their enemies eliminated in one mass destruction. Banished forever. How delightful!

The trouble was, the Kai-Via chasing the group to the camp might be caught in the process. If they followed the rebels too closely into the camp, they would also die. There was nothing he could do about it. He only had enough power to save himself.

However, Kai-Via members were replaceable. That's why they all wore black robes. They were interchangeable. Except him. Even if Stryker didn't know that before, he would soon.

Roar flopped over, and Dax let him stay that way. He would get uncomfortable and right himself. No more letting Roar slow him down.

He had to get to the camp before they started rescuing people. Besides, he knew something that no one knew that he knew.

Once again, Dax flushed with pleasure. Knowing more than anyone else was part of the game and the only way to win it, and he was going to win, without a doubt.

None of the Mages attempting the rescue were aware that he knew about the wizard. Not only that, Dax knew who he was. He and Tarek had a history together. Today he would end it, once and for all.

****

Leon glanced at the sky. It looked like another storm was coming. He hoped it wasn't one of those monster storms like the one they had a few days before. They popped up out of nowhere these days. It was as if nature was trying to rid itself of what humankind was doing to each other.

Sometimes Leon wondered if it would be better if nature won. Did Thamon really need people? Tarek said that yes, it did. But Leon wondered if his cousin was too optimistic. Perhaps being a wizard did that.

When they were younger, Leon wanted to be like Tarek, a Mage. Instead, he was Ordinary, and all his skills were something he learned and worked hard for.

Sure, Tarek said that was true about Mages, too. They had to learn what they were doing and practice. Lots of practice. At the moment Leon didn't want to be a Mage anyway. Thamon was too dangerous for them. But then it was also hazardous for Ordinaries who could resist the garbage that Aaron and his followers preached. Ordinaries like him and Samis and his group of people.

As the wind whipped through the trees behind the cabin, Leon noticed the sky to the west was darkening. This storm would hit them first and then move towards the prison camp in Hetale. Would Tarek be able to transport everyone in a storm, or would they be trapped in Dax's destruction? Leon knew that Tarek was capable of many things, but this might be too difficult.

Either way, he and his men needed to be prepared. Vald hadn't returned yet, although Silke had stopped by to let Leon know that Vald was weak, but safe, with Samis. But still, that left him with only seven men to make sure the prisoners were tucked back into the safety of the cave.

A massive clap of thunder made the cabin shake. It was time for him and his men to get to the cave opening and wait for Tarek.

However, if it rained too hard too fast, the water could rise too high for them to take a boat through. That meant that Tarek would have to transport the prisoners by himself into the cave. That was something neither of them had thought they would have to do. Leon didn't even know if it was possible.

And if Dax discovered what they were doing, he would try and find where Tarek was taking them. Leon and his men were the prisoner's and the rebel's protection. They couldn't fail now.

Fifty-Four

Meg had the strangest sensation as they flew over Dax and Roar, and as the three of them came to rest outside the prison camp. After a moment's hesitation, she decided to say what was on her mind.

"I don't think this is going to work," Meg said.

Ruth turned to Meg and asked, "Which part, and why not?"

"All of it. How can Tarek get all these prisoners out of here, and how are we going to convince Dax that the prisoners are still here? We can transform ourselves into looking like prisoners, but not enough of them. Roar will have to convince him the camp is full. Besides, I think Dax knows what we are doing."

"Of course he does," Wren answered. "That's why we are being so obvious. But he, like you, thinks we won't succeed, and that his plan to destroy the camp will destroy us too."

The three of them were waiting for Silke to let them know when Dax was almost there. Or at least that's what Meg thought that they were doing. Now it seemed as if she didn't know what was happening at all.

"So, we aren't imitating prisoners?"

"We are. But Dax will know it's us. However, Roar will

still create an illusion that makes Dax think he is also seeing all the prisoners. Then, Dax will set off his device to trigger the earthquake, thinking that he killed all the remaining Mages and us at the same time. It will give us breathing room as we plan what to do next to free all the people of Thamon from the rule of Aaron-Lem."

"But this valley will be destroyed," Meg said.

"Yes, it will change. It will be something different. Perhaps even more beautiful in the end," Ruth responded.

Meg looked at her two new friends. Not new. First. The first friends she ever had, or at least she thought that what was happening between them was what people meant by friendship. Maybe it was friendship with all of the rebels. They all worked together, each doing what they did best. They were a team. Was that friendship?

It was certainly different than what she thought she had wanted. She had thought she wanted the freedom to do and be whatever she wanted to be, without obligations to anyone. Now she was obligated to save people she didn't even know. All because the portal maker decided to banish her, instead of doing what she asked of him.

She was so engrossed in her thinking, Meg missed Silke's arrival, looking a little out of breath, her feathered hair sticking out more than usual.

"Sorry for the rush, but we need to move quickly. Dax is just over the rise. Get into place. The storm that is coming is a bad one. We had to speed up the evacuations of the prisoners before the cave flooded. We only have a few people left. Keep Dax distracted while we get the last ones out. After that, you know what to do."

Meg did know, and she still couldn't get it out of her mind that it might not work. Now that a storm was coming, she was even more worried. She hadn't told the others, but it wasn't just night time that shut down her magic.

It had happened in the last storm, too. Meg had managed to hide it before, but if it got too dark, she wouldn't be able to shapeshift to keep herself safe. But now wasn't the time to tell anyone. The rebels were counting on her.

With a flick of her hair, Silke disappeared. Giving each other a thumbs up, Wren, Meg, and Ruth headed to their positions inside the cages at the front of the prison. It was Roar's job to force the picture into Dax's mind that the prison was full, even though the guards were missing.

How long he could hold that picture, even Roar hadn't been able to tell them. Meg was praying that it was long enough to get Dax to do what he was planning, so they could all get out of there before the earthquake.

She knew that the storm would probably block her powers, but it might also work in her favor. Dax might be in a rush to get the whole thing over with quickly and not notice what was wrong in the camp.

****

Dax could feel the storm moving quickly behind him, and he was worried. These storms had become dangerous. Normally, he would have taken shelter. But how was he going to trigger the earthquake if he was hiding from a storm?

There was no way he was going to make it to the prison before the storm arrived. He didn't have to look to know that it was almost on top of them.

A blast of wind whipped through the forest as a bolt of lightning leaped from the sky and hit a tree just in front of them, barely missing the cart. The thunder that followed shook the ground so hard that Dax wondered if it would trigger the earthquake without any help from him.

If it did, Dax needed to know that the prisoners were still in the camp and that the Mages were also there trying to rescue them.

Another bolt of lightning, and Dax decided it was time to run. He could either run back through the storm towards the Temple or run to the prison and do what he came to do. He decided on the prison.

Dragging Roar by the arm, Dax took off towards the prison, the two of them dodging fallen branches as they ran. By the time they reached the prison, the lower part of the valley had already started to fill with water. The rain was coming down so fast there wasn't enough time for the water to drain away.

Dax knew that flooding happened in the last storm, and a few prisoners had drowned because their cages had been on the lower level of the prison.

If he was going to set off the earthquake, he wouldn't have time to check each cage, but he could see the form of prisoners huddled in the first ones. Even if they were only the shapeshifters, he didn't care. He wanted them dead, too.

As the rain beat down on him, Dax let go of Roar. He knew where Roar would go. He would try and save the prisoners, but it would be too late.

As Roar ran towards the prison, Dax lifted his wrist, revealing the wrist band and shot a laser beam at the tower he had filled with explosives.

Below the tower was a tunnel that connected to all the holes the prisoners had drilled into the earth, each one filled with explosives. There would be a chain reaction that would destroy everything.

The tower exploded at the same time as another bolt of lightning flashed and ground-shattering thunder ripped through the air.

As Dax ran from the camp, he laughed. The storm was helping his illusion that the camp had been destroyed by natural forces. No one would suspect that he had triggered the explosion.

No one would question whether or not it was a natural disaster. It was all working out perfectly in his favor proving once again, that if there were gods, they were on his side.

Fifty-Five

Roar ran towards the cages, just as Dax wanted him to do. He knew what he was doing. He was following the plan, making it look as if they all died in the explosion.

As he ran, Roar was grateful that he hadn't needed to project an illusion for Dax, because just running was draining all of his strength.

Even as Dax dragged him off the cart and towards the prison, Roar hadn't been sure he would be able to project the illusion that they had planned.

The storm had saved him. It produced enough chaos that Dax didn't care to see all of the prisoners. Without checking the cages, Dax had triggered the explosion just as they had wanted him to.

Now all Roar needed to do was get out of the sight of Dax, shift into a bird, and fly out of there. Roar knew that Wren, Ruth, and Meg were doing the same thing.

He hoped that they had seen Dax leaving and were already on their way. They had agreed to meet back at the cave where Tarek and Silke had taken the other Mages. It would be hard flying, but at least they would be off the ground as the earthquake hit.

Roar reached the cages, and seeing that they were empty, sighed in relief. Everyone was gone. It was time for him to leave. However, before he could shift, the earth beneath his feet started to move, knocking him over.

Still out of breath from running, Roar struggled to sit up. He watched in horror as the stone walls of the prison began to fall apart.

He was too late. It was over. The floor dropped out from under him, taking him with it. As Roar hit the ground, the rest of the wall crumbled and fell on top of him. Within seconds Roar was buried under a pile of rubble.

He didn't feel a thing.

****

Ibris quickly finished his talk with the words that he always used, "Imagine yourself within the glory of Aaron-Lem's blessings."

They were the only words that were needed this time. The crowd's minds would do the rest. It was good that he had trained them well. He didn't have time for more.

Ibris could see the storm moving across the Arrow. It was going to be another bad one, and the people needed to get to safety. And he knew that Dax was out there, and so was Stryker, along with three of the Seven.

For the first time, there were only three of the Kai-Via standing behind him. The crowd had murmured at first seeing that Kai-Via were missing. Ibris quieted them with a story that the missing Kai-Via were preparing something special for the converted.

But he knew differently. They were out in the storm. He could let them perish, or he could save them. But if he chose to rescue them, he had to do it in a way that never revealed his secret.

Even though he was pretending that he had a choice, Ibris knew that he didn't. He would not be able to live with himself if he let any more people die when he could save them. No matter who they were.

His heart was already broken in pieces by what he had done in the past. He had participated in banishing magic. The destruction that resulted from that banishment would always be eating away at his soul.

Preaching was the only way he knew how to keep everyone safe from Aaron and his warriors he had waiting in the wings should the peaceful conversion fail.

However, in this case, preaching would not save them from the storm. He would have go do it.

Who to save first, though? And how?

****

Meg crouched in terror beside a fallen tree. She had been right. Her powers were gone. She couldn't shapeshift out of this, and she had no idea which way to run to be safe.

With every flash of lightning and monstrous thunder, she became more afraid. Covering her ears helped with the noise, but not with the drenching rain, or the knowledge that one way or another, an earthquake was on the way.

For a moment, she flashed back to her dream of bodies fighting their way out of the water and realized that it had been her drowning.

Was that going to happen now? Yes, it was flooding, but how could it flood enough for her to drown?

Then she remembered the lake. What if the earthquake

broke open the space between the lake and the prison camp, or it overflowed?

Something caught her eye. Roar. He was running towards the cages. Maybe he could help get her out, but it would have to be quick. If Roar was free, that meant that Dax was ready to set off the quake.

The explosion split the air as she ran towards Roar.

For a brief moment, Meg thought that they might make it, but then the earth shuddered, and she watched the prison crumble where Roar had just been.

"No!" Meg shouted and began running towards where she had last seen him. If there had been time, she would have wondered when she had become more worried about someone other than herself. But at that moment, all she could think about was not letting Roar die. He was her friend. Ruth might never recover if Roar didn't return.

All that passed swiftly through her mind as she stumbled through the dark and rubble. She had no idea how she would get them both out of there, but she would.

The last thing Meg heard was the crack of a tree. She looked up in time to see a tree heading straight towards her, and then everything went dark.

Meg didn't see the massive wall of water that burst into the valley, the earthquake having opened a passageway from the lake. The dark water spread out, filling the holes dug by the prisoners and cracks caused by the earthquake.

As the water rose, it weakened the ground beneath the now broken prison, and it started to sink. Neither Roar nor Meg knew anything about it, which was for the best.

It would be a painless death for both of them.

Fifty-Six

The cave was filled with the sound of moaning and crying, mixed with a quiet feeling of jubilation. The prisoners were sick and in pain, but they were free. Barely.

The water in the cave had risen to the bottom of the ledge where Leon and his men had constructed shelters higher up near the back wall of the cave. They would be safe from the water and from Dax and the Kai-Via. At least for now.

Tarek was standing on the edge of the ledge, Silke on his shoulder, looking towards where he knew the opening of the cave should be. But there was nothing to see. No light filtered through, no lake was visible.

Water filled the entire opening. There was no way in, and no way out. However, even though they were trapped until the water receded, it would have been alright, except that they weren't all there. Two of their own were missing.

Wren and Ruth had managed to fly close to the ceiling of the cave and make it to the ledge before the opening closed completely. But Roar and Meg had not returned.

Ruth huddled with Wren keeping watch for their friends. Both of them were openly weeping, feeling responsible for not making sure that Roar and Meg were safe before they had gone.

Tarek knew it wouldn't do any good to remind them once again that they had done the right thing. If they hadn't left when they did, they wouldn't be here either, and they were needed.

The Mages were going to require a lot of care to recover, and Wren and Ruth could be instrumental in that. But nothing he said right now would comfort them.

Truthfully, nothing he could say to himself right now would comfort him either. Roar was a valuable member of their team, and Tarek felt responsible for the decision that had sent Roar off into Dax's clutches in the first place. If Roar didn't return, he would never forgive himself, no matter how many people told him that it was the right decision.

But what made it worse was Meg was missing too. And that was forcing him to admit to himself that Meg had become more to him than he had ever thought could happen. If she didn't return, he would never know what those feelings might become.

So he told himself to stop it. He was a wizard, after all. He wasn't supposed to doubt or be discouraged. People looked to him to solve problems and save people. But he was as trapped in the cave as everyone else. He would have to trust that somehow Meg and Roar would be alright. But how, he had no idea, because by now the valley would have been destroyed, and nothing would be able to survive that.

****

Samis dragged Vald towards the boat he kept hidden on Hetale. He knew that the Arrow would be underwater and his only way get to Woald would be by the sea. He wasn't worried about anyone seeing them.

There was no one in the Temple after Dax left to go to the prison camp, taking Roar with him. There was nothing anyone could do for Roar. Samis could only hope that the plan to rescue the prisoners had gone off without any problems.

They were only halfway to the boat when Samis and Vald were thrown to the ground. Samis knew what it was. Dax had managed to set off the earthquake.

Please let them be safe, Samis kept mumbling to himself. He was thinking of his own team of rebels as well as Roar, Meg, Ruth, and Wren. If everyone made it through this night, they might have a chance to stop Aaron from completing his plan to banish all magic from Thamon. That is, if the plan worked and no one died in the process.

Vald was doing his best to help Samis drag him towards the boat. Thanks to Silke, everything that had happened in Dax's torture room was hazy. He hoped he never remembered.

Vald knew that Silke had also saved him from feeling the pain that Dax inflicted, but now that what she had done was wearing off, he could barely keep himself from screaming. The bottom of his feet were shredded, and he knew that he was leaving a trail of blood. It didn't matter. The rain would wash it all away.

Samis kept whispering words of encouragement, telling Vald that once they were on the boat, they would be safe. They would wait for the storm to move off and then head to Woald and the deserted building.

Samis knew if his team hadn't been caught in the earthquake, they would find a place to be safe on Hetale. But Vald's friends would want to see that he was safe. Besides, maybe Silke would be at the building, and she could help with healing Vald.

But first, they had to get to the boat. The only good part of the storm was that there was no one around but them. It was not safe to be out in it. But it was safer than staying in the

Temple until Dax got back. *Anything is safer than that,* Samis thought.

Perhaps Dax would get caught in the storm and never return. Samis doubted that would happen, but one could only hope.

Fifty-Seven

At the last minute, Ibris was released from his decision to save the members of his Kai-Via. Just as he was preparing to leave, all three of the Kai-Via stumbled into the Temple.

The two Kai-Via who had followed Samis' group went off to their rooms, dripping water over the temple floor, trying not to look at Ibris to see how he felt about them not being there for the service. Ibris let them go.

He could discipline them later when he felt angry instead of relieved. Instead, he gave them a look that he hoped displayed his displeasure and turned back to Dax.

Even though the walls of the Temple were closed to keep out the storm, it was still shaking from the pounding rain and shattering thunder. However, Ibris wasn't worried now. They all knew that they could go below with the hidden pool if it were necessary. But now that everyone was back, Ibris had a feeling the storm would soon move out over the ocean.

Theses storms were getting worse, and he was sure that it wouldn't be long before they would experience another. Maybe even a worse one.

Ibris knew that what they were doing was angering nature, and sooner or later nature would eliminate all of them unless he stopped Aaron and Stryker from finishing their dream of enslaving all the people of Thamon.

Dax didn't bother hiding his excitement. He had done what Stryker had asked him to do, and he was happy to declare it to anyone, especially Ibris. After all, they were all followers of Aaron-Lem. All of them wanted all the Mages to die. He had accomplished that.

Not only were the prisoners gone, so were the Mages that were helping them escape, swallowed up in an earthquake that was helped along by the storm. It proved to Dax that he was on the side of the gods. Otherwise, why the storm?

Yes, he knew that Aaron was a manufactured God, but it served his purpose to support him. It was important for his long term plan to stay on the side of the most influential people, whoever they were.

For now, it was Aaron and Stryker. Until it wasn't, he would obey them. However, there were other gods, and those gods were on his side. It was obvious. They had helped him destroy his enemies and made him look good in front of those who owned the power.

For now. His time would come soon enough.

****

Dax continued to strut his success in front of Ibris. He was tempting him, trying to provoke him into a response. Dax wanted Ibris to give away the fact that he was upset about what Dax had done to the prisoners.

Dax wanted to prove, to himself at least, that Ibris was not really on Aaron's side, that he was not a believer in Aaron-Lem. But Ibris disappointed him. Again.

Instead, Ibris remained the Preacher. Calm and serene,

smiling as if he was happy at what Dax had done. If Ibris wasn't pleased, he wasn't showing it.

Once Dax realized that Ibris was not going to give him what he wanted, he decided to celebrate his success somewhere else. There was no point in wasting this moment on a losing battle.

Sooner or later he would find Ibris' weak spot. For now, it was time to have some fun. Later, after the storm passed, he would have to go below and deal with that dead guy. Right now, he was going to celebrate with one, or maybe more, of the women that Aaron had gifted him.

Yes, Aaron took good care of him, Dax thought. It would be a shame to have to destroy him. But when the time came, Aaron would understand, even while hating Dax for it, because Aaron understood the pull of power.

So although Aaron would fight to the end, he would die knowing why Dax did it.

But that was a long way away. For now, he had done the first thing he wanted in his plan, and it had worked out perfectly. When the time was right, he would make his move.

****

After Dax went to his room, Ibris sat alone in the Temple, watching the storm move out to sea. In the evil part of his mind, Ibris wished that Stryker had perished in the storm.

It would have been easier to let the storm take care of the Stryker problem. But Ibris had chosen what he believed had been the right thing to do.

Without Stryker's knowledge, Ibris had cleared the path home from the cave for him.

Now, in his mind's eye, Ibris could see Stryker wet, but safe, in his room. It was a dangerous thing for him to enter Stryker's thoughts, and he withdrew as soon as he knew Stryker was safe.

Yes, perhaps it would have been better to let Stryker be caught in the storm because Stryker had found the first part of the pendant.

Perhaps it had been somewhat disappointing to find only one part of the pendant. Ibris knew there were three parts. How he knew about the necklace and why it was in three parts was something he had kept to himself all these years. He knew that he would have to tell the whole story to someone soon, if he was going to get help to stop Stryker from finding the whole thing.

Because now that Stryker had found the first section, he was one step closer to having the ability to project thoughts and ideas without anyone being able to stop him.

Ibris knew he couldn't let that happen. Sooner or later, he would have to find the rebels and work with them. When he had seen Stryker's face as he emerged from the cave, Ibris knew that it would have to be sooner.

Although Stryker was trying to hide his happiness, he couldn't conceal the self-satisfied smirk that played around his mouth. Yes, Stryker was dripping wet and shivering. But Ibris suspected that the shivering was not from the cold, but excitement. Stryker had found the top third of the pendant. That changed everything.

Fifty-Eight

Meg thought she was dreaming again. But this time it felt
so real. It was unbelievably cold. So cold, she could feel herself
shaking and hear herself moaning.

This is new, she thought. In her dreams, she had never
cried out loud. When something bumped up against her, Meg
screamed and then started to gag as water flowed into her
mouth.

That had never happened before, either. Coughing and
spitting the water out, she thrashed looking for what had
bumped into her. A flash of lightning showed her that it had
only been a log floating by.

Confused, she thought, *A log? Why a log? Where am I?*

Another lightning flash revealed a vast expanse of water
surrounding her. There was nothing else to see. Where was she?
How had she gotten here?

Disoriented, Meg spun around and around in the water,
arms flaying and legs kicking trying to keep her mouth above
the waterline, wondering if even in a dream one could actually
drown.

Slowly she remembered that she had been running towards
Roar as the building fell on top of him. Everything came

rushing back, and she screamed, "Roar!" taking in another swallow of water. Spitting and sputtering, legs kicking wildly underwater, Meg turned around and around looking for him. There was nothing. Just a black open expanse of water, the surface boiling from drenching rain.

No, she wasn't dreaming now, but she remembered her dream. In the dream, she was helpless. Was she helpless now? If only she could turn into a fish or something that swam, she could find Roar. But she couldn't. It was too dark. She had no magic. She had no abilities at all.

In her mind, she thought she heard someone say, "But that doesn't mean you can't save him."

No, it doesn't, Meg said to herself. But where was he? Thinking that he might be floating underwater since the last time she saw him he was under a pile of rocks, she started diving beneath the water looking for him.

It was so dark that Meg couldn't even see her own legs kicking beneath the water. But she didn't stop. Each time Meg rose to the surface to take a breath, she was even more exhausted. But she refused to give in, though part of her thought that it was too late. How long had he been underwater?

Meg dove over and over again, reaching out in the dark to find Roar. Mostly she found nothing, but once in a while, her hands caught something, but it was never Roar.

Overcoming her distaste for touching whatever she was finding as she searched, she kept going. Even if he were dead, she would find him and bring him back to the others. Especially to Ruth, who Meg knew cherished him.

The last time she rose, she could barely breathe. Even if it hadn't been dark, she still wouldn't have been able to see. Her eyesight was failing. Her breath was failing. She had failed. She had run away. She was a failure in every sense of the word.

A log bumped into her again, and she held on without thinking, and then once again, everything went black.

****

Meg woke with a start. Her head was pounding, and she was freezing. Perhaps she had died because she could feel herself flying through the air. Not flying. Pulled, lifted. It hurt. She closed her eyes, and everything went black again.

The next time she opened her eyes, it was still dark, but now she was warm. Carefully moving her head to the side, she saw Roar lying on his back, covered with a blanket. Was he dead? How did they get here? Where were they?

Struggling to sit up, her head splitting with each movement, she screamed. What she was seeing wasn't possible. Then she stopped screaming and starting crying.

"How?" she managed to say.

"Sh… go back to sleep," her sister said. Looking over at Roar, Suzanne added. "You're both safe now."

Fifty-Nine

It was days later before the story of what happened could be told. The storm had passed, and the sun was shining once again. The Mages who had been prisoners were still in the cave, but most of them were recovering and would soon be able to participate in planning for the future.

Vald and Samis had found Roar, Meg, and her sister, Suzanne, at the deserted building. The next day, the five of them slowly made their way to the cabin. Suzanne could have flown them there one at a time, but a dragon flying would have been too dangerous for all of them.

For the most part, Roar and Meg had recovered, but neither of them talked about what had happened. Mostly because they couldn't remember much. They were waiting for Suzanne to fill them in.

Vald was still weak, his feet not fully healed. Leon and Samis had not left his side, doing everything they could to ease his pain and heal his body and his spirit.

Even though Vald assured them that he was fine, they were all keeping a careful watch on him. After what had happened to him, they all wondered if he would ever fully recover.

Samis' group of rebels had turned around once the storm

began and they hoped that Dax thought they had drowned. All of them were now back in Woald reinventing themselves as if they were staunch supporters of Aaron-Lem. When the time was right, Samis would call on them again.

Sitting in the cabin, everyone now safe, Tarek couldn't keep his eyes off the two sisters that were sitting across the cabin from him. No one could. They were all waiting to hear how Meg's sister, Suzanne, had managed to save Meg and Roar from the rising waters. Where had she come from? Suzanne said she would tell the story once everyone felt better.

Now was the time. Except they had to wait for Silke, who said she had an errand to run. While they waited, Tarek thought about his feelings for Meg. He knew he had them, but he wasn't sure what that meant, or what he could do about them.

He had happily lived alone for most of his life. Now there was not only Meg, but there were also all these other people. There were the rescued who were hiding in the cave, Samis' rebels, and then all the people sitting with him, crowded together in the cabin.

Tarek wasn't sure he liked that he was surrounded by so many people who were counting on him. But at the moment he couldn't do anything about it.

A second later, Silke was on his shoulder, looking pleased with herself. Tarek wondered what she had been up to, but since it was apparent she wasn't going to tell, he turned his attention to Suzanne, and said, "I think we're ready to hear what happened."

"There's not much to tell," Suzanne said.

Meg reached over and grabbed her hand, surprising both herself and Suzanne. Although sisters in the Realm called Erda, they had never been close. Meg had thought that Suzanne was an idiot for spending her life taking care of other people, being an ambassador between the Earth and Erda dimensions. While Suzanne worked, Meg wasted time. Suzanne lived driven by purpose, and Meg had believed anyone who didn't play all the time was an idiot.

"I used to think you were a fool, Suzanne," Meg said. "But now I realize that I resented you and the life you had made for yourself. I told myself that you were a fool because I was jealous. Everyone loved you. I thought myself better than you because you can only shapeshift into one thing, a dragon, and I could be anyone.

"I thought that the fact that I could be more than you made me better than you, that it made me free to do whatever I wanted to do. But I have learned so much being here with these people. Things I never thought I would know, let alone want to know."

As Meg spoke, she risked a glance at Tarek. Something was happening with him, and maybe with her, but he ignored her, so she turned back to Suzanne, squeezing her hand.

"I never thought I would see you again, Suzanne, and based on how I used to treat you, I never thought you would bother to come to find me. But you did. You saved me. You saved us. Why? And how? How did you find me?"

Suzanne squeezed Meg's hand back. If she was surprised to see how much Meg had changed, she didn't show it.

"It wasn't that hard. It just took time. After we realized that you were gone, and not just pretending to run away, I started looking. It took me a little while to realize that you weren't on Erda at all, and the only thing I could think of that happened is that you left through a portal.

"There aren't that many portal makers on Erda. I eventually tracked down the one that you used. But at first, he wouldn't tell me where he had sent you. Eventually, he confessed that he didn't send you where you had asked to go but instead had banished you to someplace dangerous for shapeshifters.

"Once he told me that, I forced him to send me here, too."

"How long have you been here?" Leon asked. "And how did you find Meg and Roar?"

"Not long. But long enough to learn about Aaron-Lem and what Aaron has done, and wants to do, with the people of Thamon. Long enough to know to follow Dax to find out what he was doing. Long enough to be glad that I came. Not only to rescue you and Roar, but to be part of your rebellion. And perhaps meet another dragon or two in the process. If there are any left."

Meg turned and hugged her sister. There was time enough to tell her that she no longer was able to be anyone. That at night, she was Ordinary.

Meg looked around the cabin and at the mix of Mages and Ordinary and realized that she called them all friends. That together, they were strong. Strong enough to save the prisoners, and sooner or later, strong enough to rescue the rest of Thamon.

They were not going to be banished. If anyone was, it was going to be the rulers of Aaron-Lem. But for now, they were safe, and Meg was happy. Perhaps that was the real freedom.

Sixty

Later that day, Tarek and Suzanne sat on the ledge inside of the cave swinging their legs. The water had receded, returning the cave to a safe and private space.

Leon and his men had turned the room behind the ledge into something almost cozy. Water had stopped dripping down on the prisoners. Fires burned in front of the tents that they had erected for each family. There were not many of them left.

Even after the rescue, some of the people had still died. Their experience had been so much worse than Tarek could have imagined, and they had lost the energy or heart to recover. Although there had been hundreds of Mages on the Islands before the Kai-Via had arrived. Now there were less than a few dozen.

Tarek shook his head. Now was not the time to be thinking about the cruelty that Dax had enjoyed at the expense of these people. Now was the time to listen to what Suzanne had to tell him. What hadn't she told them yet? Would it help in the future?

But instead of sharing those ideas, Suzanne began to tell him more about Meg and their life together, and Tarek discovered that was what he really wanted to hear. Suzanne smiled as she spoke. She couldn't help herself. Now that her sister was growing into someone everyone admired, Suzanne told herself that she knew it would happen all along.

Except she hadn't. She had only prayed that it would.

Tarek listened with his whole heart. Suzanne liked that about him. But she knew that there was a story he hadn't told anyone yet. Actually, there were stories that many of them hadn't revealed yet. But time would take care of that.

Besides, Silke said that she had found them something they could use in the fight to free Thamon. Whatever that was, she was keeping that a secret, too. It was probably for the best. Right now, they all needed more time to recover.

Suzanne realized that she had received something she never thought she would find when she came after her sister to rescue her. She had found a family of like-minded souls. Here, on another planet, there was a community and friendship. It was good to think that she could call this planet home.

Because what she had not told anyone, including her sister, was that there was no way to go back. She and Meg were here on Thamon to stay.

****

Months later ...

Meg and Tarek stood in the back of the chapel listening to the Preacher. Ruth had transformed their faces, and with masked minds, they looked like one of the converted.

Hidden beneath their black robes, their fingers touched. Now, even more than ever, they were sure of their mission. Restore Thamon's people to themselves. Magic was not dead. And they were not alone.

After Banished, What's Next?

Join me in the next book in this series, *Betrayed*. There are so many questions that need to be answered!

Who is betrayed, and why? What happens between Meg and Tarek? Where are the other parts of the pendant? Who hid it in the first place? What is Wren's story? What did Silke find? Where did Tarek come from? How are all these people related?

So many stories to come…

Thank you for joining me in this one!

Love, Beca

PS

Be the first to know when there are new books, Join my mailing list at becalewis.com/fantasy and get the free short story that answers so many questions about how the Karass, Erda, and Thamon series are related. Yes, Suzanne is in all of them. How is that possible?

Author's Note

During my childhood, every summer, a group of Steelworkers from Pittsburgh would come to Penn State in State College, PA, and my dad would be one of their instructors.

At the end of the session, there would always be a picnic at a place called Penn's Cave in Center Hall, PA.

As the grownups talked and played baseball, I needed, as always, to get away by myself. So I would escape the heat and the crowds and take the boat trip through Penn's Cave.

I loved walking down the path to the cave where the heat of the day transformed into a cool magical place. Inside the cave, the guide described what we were seeing, shining lights on them, and later transforming the caverns with blue, red, and green lights. I would let my imagination roam. We were no longer on earth. We were someplace else.

The cave opened into a lake where a swan would be swimming. The transformation from the dark, cold, wet cave into the light, the beautiful lake, the swan with its grace, would be the spark that kept me coming back year after year.

Although the cave is much more a tourist attraction now than the hidden cave of my youth, even as an adult I have visited every chance I get, dragging friends and family with me.

As the muse would have it, as I was writing this book, the cave popped up in my head, and I had to put it in. Then magically, it turned out that my family all decided to visit the cave.

Some for the first time. When my teenage grandson said, "I love this," it all came full circle.

So the cave had to be in this book. Magic, right under our feet. And yes, it really is 350 million years old. And no, I can't comprehend that.

******

Connect with me online:
Twitter: http://twitter.com/becalewis
Facebook: https://www.facebook.com/becalewiscreative
Pinterest: https://www.pinterest.com/theshift/
Instagram: http://instagram.com/becalewis
LinkedIn: https://linkedin.com/in/becalewis

ACKNOWLEDGMENTS

I could never write a book without the help of my friends and my book community. Thank you Jet Tucker, Jamie Lewis, Diana Cormier, and Heidi Christianson for taking the time to do the final reader proof. You can't imagine how much I appreciate it.

A huge thank you to Laura Moliter for her fantastic book editing.

Thank you to the fabulous Molly Phipps at wegotyoucoveredbookdesign.com for the beautiful book covers for the *Erda* series.

Thank you to every other member of my Book Community who help me make so many decisions that help the book be the best book possible.

Thank you to all the people who tell me that they love to read these stories. Those random comments from friends and strangers are more valuable than gold.

And always, thank you to my beloved husband, Del, for being my daily sounding board, for putting up with all my questions, my constant need to want to make things better, and for being the love of my life, in more than just this one lifetime.

OTHER BECA BOOKS

The Karass Chronicles - Magical Realism
Karass, Pragma, Jatismar, Exousia, Stemma, Paragnosis

The Return To Erda Series - Fantasy
Shatterskin, Deadsweep, Abbadon

The Chronicles of Thamon - Fantasy
Banished, Betrayed, Discovered

The Shift Series - Spiritual Self-Help
Living in Grace: The Shift to Spiritual Perception
The Daily Shift: Daily Lessons From Love To Money
The 4 Essential Questions: Choosing Spiritually Healthy Habits
The 28 Day Shift To Wealth: A Daily Prosperity Plan
The Intent Course: Say Yes To What Moves You
Imagination Mastery: A Workbook For Shifting Your Reality

Perception Parables: - Fiction - very short stories
Love's Silent Sweet Secret: A Fable About Love
Golden Chains And Silver Cords: A Fable About Letting Go

Advice: - Nonfiction
A Woman's ABC's of Life: Lessons in Love, Life and Career from Those Who Learned The Hard Way

ABOUT BECA LEWIS

Beca writes books that she hopes will change people's perceptions of themselves and the world, and open possibilities to things and ideas that are waiting to be seen and experienced.

At sixteen, Beca founded her own dance studio. Later, she received a Master's Degree in Dance in Choreography from UCLA and founded the Harbinger Dance Theatre, a multimedia dance company, while continuing to run her dance school.

After graduating—to better support her three children—Beca switched to the sales field, where she worked as an employee and independent contractor to many industries, excelling in each while perfecting and teaching her Shift® system, and writing books.

She joined the financial industry in 1983 and became an Associate Vice President of Investments at a major stock brokerage firm, and was a licensed Certified Financial Planner for more than twenty years.

This diversity, along with a variety of life challenges, helped fuel the desire to share what she's learned by writing and talking with the hope that it will make a difference in other people's lives.

Beca grew up in State College, PA, with the dream of becoming a dancer and then a writer. She carried that dream forward as she fulfilled a childhood wish by moving to Southern

California in 1969. Beca told her family she would never move back to the cold.

After living there for thirty years, she met her husband Delbert Lee Piper, Sr., at a retreat in Virginia, and everything changed. They decided to find a place they could call their own which sent them off traveling around the United States. For a year or so they lived and worked in a few different places before returning to live in the cold once again near Del's family in a small town in Northeast Ohio, not too far from State College.

When not working and teaching together, they love to visit and play with their combined family of eight children and five grandchildren, read, study, do yoga or taiji, feed birds, work in their garden, and design things. Actually, designing things is what Beca loves to do. Del enjoys the end result.

CPSIA information can be obtained
at www.ICGtesting.com
Printed in the USA
LVHW051706060320
649227LV00008B/456